THE CLIQUE
SUMMER COLLECTION

MASSIE

CLIQUE novels by Lisi Harrison:

THE CLIQUE
BEST FRIENDS FOR NEVER
REVENGE OF THE WANNABES
INVASION OF THE BOY SNATCHERS
THE PRETTY COMMITTEE STRIKES BACK
DIAL L FOR LOSER
IT'S NOT EASY BEING MEAN
SEALED WITH A DISS
BRATFEST AT TIFFANY'S

THE CLIQUE SUMMER COLLECTION:
MASSIE
DYLAN (Coming May 6)
ALICIA (Coming June 3)
KRISTEN (Coming July 1)
CLAIRE (Coming August 5)

THE CLIQUE
SUMMER COLLECTION
MASSIE

A CLIQUE NOVEL BY
LISI HARRISON

poppy

LITTLE, BROWN AND COMPANY
New York   Boston

"Glamorous" by William Adams, Christopher Brian Bridges, Stacy Ferguson, Jamal F.
Jones, Elvis Williams, Jr. (Cherry River Music Co., Elvis Lee Music, EMI April Music Inc.,
EMI Blackwood Music, Inc., Headphone Junkie Publishing, Ludacris Universal Publishing,
Showdy Pimp Music, Universal Music Corp., Will I Am Music). All rights reserved.

Poppy

Little, Brown and Company
Hachette Book Group USA
237 Park Avenue, New York, NY 10017
For more of your favorite series, go to www.pickapoppy.com

First Edition: April 2008

The Poppy name and logo are trademarks of Hachette Book Group USA.

Cover design by Andrea C. Uva
Cover and author photos by Roger Moenks

alloy**entertainment**

Produced by Alloy Entertainment
151 West 26th Street, New York, NY 10001

ISBN: 978-0-316-02751-9

10 9 8 7 6 5 4 3 2 1
CWO
Printed in the United States of America

For Josh Bank, Sara Shandler, and Lanie Davis. Our love child has arrived!
Thanks for your tireless work and for not killing me along the way. ☺

The morning sun felt like a spotlight. It cast a thick yellow beam through the window in Brownie's humid, hay-filled stall, illuminating the white horse and blinding his owner. But Massie Block didn't mind one bit. She was used to the glare of the spotlight. She craved it. Chased it. Dressed for it. Basking in its warmth kept her alive. Yet today, the spotlight was threatening to shine on someone else. And Massie wanted to die.

She lowered her tortoiseshell Dior glasses and snapped a purple glitter hair elastic around the bottom of Brownie's foot-long mane braid. His intricate hairstyle, aubergine satin blinders, and gold glitter mascara were sure to impress the judges of the Galwaugh Farms Jump and Canter Competition and, more important, the editor of *Horse & Rider*.

For the first time in the equestrian magazine's history, the winning captain of the Galwaugh Farms' JACC would be featured on the glossy cover of its September issue. And what better way to kick off eighth grade at OCD than with a beautifully airbrushed alpha portrait?

Pop!

Massie jumped. The sound of her teammate Jacqueline Dyer popping Forever Fruit Stride gum between her over-bleached teeth was unnerving.

"J, can you puh-lease stop that!" Massie hissed at the dark brown wood stall wall between them. "You're scaring Brownie."

"Sah-rreee," Jacqueline called, her nasal voice slightly higher than usual. "It's a nervous thing."

"What are you so nervous about?" Massie asked, already knowing the answer. She tucked her black-and-gold Hermès cravat into the sharp V of her velvet riding vest, even though it was perfectly tucked already. It was all she could do to keep from stress-biting the black tips off her not-so-French French manicure. "Those blue ribbons have Galwaugh Goddesses written all over them."

"Unless the Mane Mamas take *first*," Whitney Bennett chimed in from behind the opposite wall.

"Impossible!" Massie barked at her summer best friends. "We win JACC every year." As team captain it was her job to keep everyone positive, even when things seemed utterly hopeless.

"Yeah, but we never had Fall-a Abdul on our team." Jacqueline set off a round of gum pops that made Brownie's gold lashes flutter in panic.

"Stop *calling* me that," Selma Gallman whined from the other side of the stable wall. "I told you, I got an inner-ear infection from swimming in the lake yesterday. And that's why I keep falling. My balance is off."

"What was your excuse last week?" Massie marched out of her stall and straight into Selma's. "Or the week before?"

She was through with the calm, confident leader act. She

lifted her Diors and glared into Selma's heavy-lidded mud-brown eyes.

"Thanks to your *ear*, my six-year winning streak is in major jeopardy." Massie's voice trembled. A vision of the highly decorated "Wins Wall" in her bedroom—between the bay window and the walk-in closet—flashed before her. It had just enough room for one last ribbon and a framed cover of *Horse & Rider.* And the thought of that space staying empty filled her amber eyes with salty pre-tears. Not only for her. Or for the Galwaugh Goddesses. But for Brownie's elegant hairstyle and all of his hard practicing.

For three exhausting weeks, Massie had focused on victory as a way to put the nightmarish end of seventh grade behind her: The Pretty Committee, with help from Layne Abeley, had accidentally punctured Briarwood's rooftop wave pool, causing the whole thing to leak and collapse, flooding the boys' school. As a result, the ex-crushes were months away from invading OCD and threatening Massie's alpha status. Add in a summer away from her best friends—Dylan spa-ing in Hawaii, Alicia partying with her cousins on the Costa del Sol in Spain, Kristin tutoring spoiled brats in Westchester, and Claire reuniting with her old Orlan-dull buddies back in Florida—and ruling Galwaugh Farms' exclusive riding camp was the only way to keep from snot-sobbing herself to sleep at night.

Glancing out the window, Massie tried to distract herself to keep from losing her cool. But the sight of junior campers, staff members, parents, and local reporters making their way to the dirt-paved arena only upset her more. The only thing worse than losing was losing in public. And thanks to Selma, she was minutes away from both.

The familiar smell of Jacqueline's citrus-scented gum and Whitney's flowery freesia hoof 'n' nail cream enveloped her. Her girls were standing beside her now in solidarity, shooting how-could-you-be-so-lame rays at Selma and Latte—her carrot-farting steed.

Whitney scraped her riding crop against the scrubbed concrete. "How *did* you qualify for our team, anyway?"

"Does it matter?" Selma took her fleshy pink hand off her cocoa horse's buttock and placed it on her own lumpy hip. "I thought the whole point of riding was to have fun."

"No, Sel-muh." Massie kicked a haystack with her black Hermès riding boots. "The whole point of riding is to win. The *fun* part is laughing at the losers."

Selma opened her heart-shaped mouth to respond but was cut off by Alessandro, their award-winning groom.

"A good-luck gift for youuuu," he announced in his sing-songy European accent.

Everyone turned to face the tall fortysomething man bounding toward them in an ivory linen suit and black Gucci loafers. He had four enormous silver gift bags swinging from the mini-biceps on his hooked fingers.

"Enjoyyyy." Alessandro smiled proudly, deepening the Botox-thirsty smile lines that fanned out from the corners of his dark eyes. His black hair was parted neatly at the side and plastered across his forehead with cherry-scented pomade. He gave each girl a bag, then stepped back to witness the joy.

Massie offered Alessandro a courteous pre-thank-you smile. But it was fake. Unless the bag contained the secret to keeping Selma on her saddle during the competition, its contents were meaningless.

"Toooo cuh-yoot." Jacqueline held up a delicious caramel leather saddle with a big *J* hand-stitched in scarlet thread across the seat. Its dangling stirrups were studded with tiny red horseshoes for luck.

"I second that." Whitney kissed her scarlet *W,* leaving behind a glossy soft pink lip print.

"Third." Selma held up three fingers.

Massie rolled her eyes as Selma fought to position her new saddle on Latte, the pink elastic band on her loose cotton underwear oozing out the top of her jodhpurs as she struggled with her straddle-mount.

"Hey, Elizabeth Hassel-buuutt," Massie snickered. "Stop torturing us with *The View*!"

"Whoa!" Whitney blurted, just like she always did when someone said something most people would simply laugh at.

Jacqueline giggled into the big yellow bubble she was blowing. It popped against her wide smile.

"Latte's skin is oily," Selma responded defensively. Her shifty eyes bore into the groom, scorching him with blame. "He wasn't greasy *before* camp started."

Alessandro patted his ultra-smooth side part. "With all due respect, Ms. Gallman, I have been show-grooming for twenty-seven years, and I have never been accused of *oily animal*. Not even during my stint with the seal theater at Sea World." He took off his ivory linen jacket and folded it across one arm, smoothing out the heat-creased sleeves with intense concentration. "Now open your gift," he urged Massie.

"Why?" She flattened the saddlebags on her olive jodhpurs. "I already know what it is."

"Yes, my dear captain." He playfully flicked the metallic bag with his buffed fingernail. "But yours is special."

Special? Massie felt her lips curl into a soft grin. She was a sucker for that word.

She lifted the silver tissue out of the bag and stuffed it in a hanging copper bucket marked GUM RAPPERS that had been incorrectly spelled by Jacqueline in Paint-The-Town-Red nail polish. Massie hadn't bothered to correct her.

"What's this?" Massie examined the new butterscotch-colored monogrammed saddle. A gold arm was fixed to the left of the cantle. She pushed the button at its base and out popped a gleaming round side-view mirror.

"To check the competition?" Whitney crinkled her freckle-dusted nose.

"No." Alessandro beamed. "The gloss."

"Whoa!" Whitney cupped the tight blond bun on the back of her head.

Massie stood on her tiptoes and threw her arms around the groom. Her vision fogged—a mix of joyous tears and a reaction to the pungent smell of his spicy deodorant. He was like the human form of comfort food. After three trying weeks with Sel-muh, this was just the pick-me-up she needed.

"Now these . . ." Jacqueline hurried to her stall and quickly returned with an armful of black velvet helmets. "I had our team name inscribed on the backs."

Massie reached for hers. Funny how ah-dorable accessories had a way of lightening even the darkest of times.

"Wait, what is *this*?" She stared at the swirling red-stitched letters that spelled *Galwaugh Girls*.

"Aren't they sweet?" Jacqueline asked as she happily handed out the rest.

"But we're the Galwaugh *Goddesses*! And have been for six summers." Massie picked at the thread to see if it was removable.

It wasn't.

Jacqueline pulled one of her tight black curls, then released it, sending it boinging back into place above her shoulder "I couldn't fit 'Goddesses' on the back," she explained. "It was too long."

"So is this day." Massie tucked a glossy strand of chestnut hair into her unsightly (but mandatory) hair net, and fastened the leather strap on her helmet with an angry snap.

Just then Lill piped in over the camp loudspeaker in her shaky old-lady voice. "Galwaugh Farms' fifty-seventh annual JACC is about to commence. Spectators, take your seats. Riders, mount your horses," instructed the head equestrian.

The Galwaugh Girls squealed with nervous delight while Massie prayed.

Instead of thanking Gawd for the usual—her ah-mazing teammates, their trusted horses, and their guaranteed spot in the winner's circle—she looked up at the dark wood rafters and stuck out her tongue. *That's for sending me Selma.*

"It's showtime." Alessandro clapped. "Everyone in formation—Whitney, Selma, Jacqueline, then Captain Massie in the rear."

"Massie in the *rear*," Whitney, Jacqueline, and Massie all repeated in a fit of laughter, just like they did every year when their groom called their procession order.

Selma rolled her droopy eyes.

"Chip-chip!" Alessandro barked his Euro version of "chop-chop" while swatting at a circling fly.

Without another word, the girls speed-glossed, buttoned their black velvet blazers, and reached for the brown suede reins on their gold-dusted horses.

Once outside, they climbed into their new saddles and joined the silent ceremonial parade of sixteen riders down the lush tree-lined path toward the arena. Galwaugh Farms had over a hundred acres of winding trails and grassy meadows, but the exclusive riding camp was on the north side of Hunter Lake, where Massie had met her on-again, off-again crush Chris Abeley almost a year ago.

The collective clip-clopping of horseshoes against the gravel synched with the rhythm of Massie's speeding heart-beat, delivering a hint of harmony to a situation that had been stressing her out for days. She took, deep cleansing breaths: *Inthroughthenose . . . aaaaand . . . outthroughthemouth . . .*

The fresh, leafy smell of a new summer and the familiar bobbing of her A-cups calmed her. Casually, she sneaked a peek at the competition in her new side-mirror. None of the other girls had coordinated helmets or saddles. Some had pimped their rides, but the yellow tulip tiara on Aspen's over-size white head and the pink polka-dot bow in Lightfoot's tangled locks were no challenge for Massie and her sparkling Galwaugh Girls. They would clean up in the style category. And surely *her* score would elevate Selma's, so . . .

A round of flashbulbs went off as they entered the holding ring—a circular pen with a sliding metal gate that led to the hurdle-filled arena. Local reporters and family members clung to the guardrails shouting good-luck wishes to their favorite riders. Massie's parents were preparing for a charity party at their house in Southampton and couldn't make it. Which was fine. Parents could be so distracting, and she had more important things to worry about.

"Over here!" called a chubby redheaded woman wearing a hunter green visor with the iconic *Horse & Rider* Clydesdale printed on the brim.

More important things, like her *Horse & Rider* cover.

Massie offered the reporter a winning grin. But before she could remove the lens cap from her Nikon, Brownie stopped suddenly, jerking Massie forward and ruining her photo op.

"Whoa!" Whitney hollered, slapping one white-gloved hand over her glossy mouth and pointing to the ground with the other.

Massie gasped.

Selma was on the ground, rolling across the dusty ring like

a wayward clump of tumbleweed stuffed in tight, oat-colored jodhpurs.

A team of medics raced toward her crumpled form.

Spectators stood. Cameras clicked. The Mane Mamas, the Giddy-Ups, and the Hot2Trots snickered. Latte stood in place, looking a little embarrassed for his rider.

Massie squeezed her suede reins until her knuckles turned white. "We're so done," she muttered, angling her body so the reporter couldn't capture her panic-sweaty forehead.

"I know what she needs." Jacqueline spit a wad of sticky yellow gum into her glove and chucked it onto Selma's saddle. "That should hold her for a while."

"Very funny," Selma said as two overdenimed female stable hands lifted her back up. She flicked the gum away with a ragged-cuticled fingertip.

Whitney and Jacqueline snickered into their white-gloved hands.

Massie wanted to laugh with the rest of her teammates but couldn't. There was no time. Her reputation, her ribbon, and her magazine cover were about to ride off into the sunset and leave her in the dirt—just like Jacqueline's chewed-up sticky wad of Forever Fruit Stride. Just like Selma's dust-covered behind every time she mounted Latte.

Unless . . .

"I forgot Brownie's face mist," Massie announced as she leaned left and tugged on his reins. "Be right back!"

"Whoa! Where are you going?" Whitney called as her captain charged toward the exit.

Alessandro urged Massie to stop—the competition was about to begin—but she ignored him. Seconds later she was tearing down the deserted trail: butt lifted, knees bent, and abs tight, two words propelling her forward—the same two words that gave her life meaning:

Number and *one*.

The well-heeled JACC spectators sprang to their pedicured feet and cheered wildly when Massie and Brownie shot back into the holding pen. Instantly, Massie's heart soared like a first-place helium balloon. So what if the applause was for someone else? Soon it would be for her.

As long as the jar tucked into her velvet blazer pocket lived up to its promise.

"Another stellar landing by Molly Gold-Starr!" Lill raved, her thin, coral-covered lips pressing against the tabletop mic in the center of the ringside judges' table.

The crowd whooped and hollered even louder.

"Bringing the Mane Mamas' scores up to a near-perfect twenty-eight out of thirty." Lill's brittle, mousy brown hair clung to her long wrinkled neck as she delivered the devastating news.

"Massie, where have you *been*?" Whitney called from the row of hitching posts, where she, Jacqueline, and Selma had been pacing the tips of their shined boots muddy.

"We're up next!" Jacqueline stuffed a fresh stick of Stride in her mouth, adding to the giant clump she was already chewing.

Massie jumped off Brownie and tied him next to the other horses.

"What's the point?" Whitney glared at Selma, who pretended not to have heard the insult.

"Shhhh." Massie covered Brownie's ears. "Animals can feel our stress."

She soothe-rubbed Brownie while tracking the four pony-tailed brunettes, who began blowing handfuls of cocky kisses to their fans while they victory-pranced out of the arena. A storm of pink, red, and white rose petals hailed down around them, practically spelling out the word *winners* as they landed in the hoof-marked dust.

"Team huddle!" Massie shouted.

Her girls formed an instant prayer circle while their horses waited dutifully in the background.

"We're going to take five and clear the field," Lill announced. "And return with our final team of the day; six-time JACC champions the Galwaugh Goddess—I mean, Galwaugh Girls."

Massie rolled her eyes at Jacqueline, silently re-reprimanding her for the helmet typo.

"Is it too late to sign up for tennis camp?" Jacqueline swallowed her gum, then immediately replaced it with a fresh piece.

"We still have a chance." Massie smirked at Selma, arching a glossy brown brow.

Instinctively, Selma took a small step back.

"A chance at third, maybe." Whitney sighed as the Mane Mamas returned to the holding ring, exchanging a round of it's-in-the-bag high fives with the stable hands, counselors, and coaches.

"Trust me." Massie grinned as she pulled the brown glass jar out of her pocket.

"Leather glue?" Jacqueline twirled another black curl.

Massie bit her glossy lower lip and nodded slowly.

"Whoa!" Whitney gasped, catching on. Her green eyes widened with a mix of amusement and disbelief.

"Come on, we have to work fast." Massie hurried over to Latte.

"Stay away from her!" Selma shouted, her voice suddenly shaky with panic.

Massie slid her black boot in the iron stirrup and lifted herself up to the saddle. Whitney and Jacqueline rushed to her side.

"Stop! Get down!" Selma tugged the back of Massie's olive pant leg. But Massie, struggling to balance in the wobbly stirrup, swatted her away like a flea.

Once stable, she unscrewed the silver top of the glass jar and lifted out a small black paintbrush. Thick, sticky glue dripped slowly off the bottom of the brush in teardrop-shaped globules. She spread the clear mixture across the entire seat, covering the red embroidered *S* with a glassy layer of the super-adhesive.

"What are you doing!?" Selma grabbed Massie's leg.

"What she should have done a long time ago." Jacqueline lunged forward and pried Selma off.

"This is illeg—!" Selma shouted. But Whitney covered her mouth and silenced her before anyone overheard.

"Ladies and gentlemen," Lill began, her piercing tone

sending a trio of nesting robins into flight overhead. "We are now ready to conclude this very exciting competition with our first rider from the Galwaugh Girls. Miss Selma Gallman!"

Soft courtesy claps welcomed her to the ring.

Massie jumped to the ground and tossed the glue bottle behind a giant poo-stack by the hitching posts. "Get awn!" she whisper-hissed to Selma.

Whitney and Jacqueline snickered into their palms.

"No way!" Selma whisper-hissed back.

Massie placed her hands on her hips. "Um, Selma, are you a talking horse?"

"No, why?" she asked.

"Then stop being a nayyyyy-sayer!"

The girls snickered again.

"Miss Selma Gallman?" Lill's voice sounded like it was personally searching the ring. The microphone crackled.

"Awn!" Massie cracked her riding crop against the ground, causing a puff of dirt to shoot up angrily. "Now!"

"Fine." Selma grabbed the stirrup bar. "But this is not over!" In one swift motion she pulled herself up. She swung her back leg around the horse but lost her footing and landed sidesaddle.

"Lift your leg!" Jacqueline snapped.

Selma's face turned bright red as she strained to move. "I can't! It's stuck!"

"Miss Selma Gallman!" Lill insisted one last time over the loudspeaker.

"Good luck!"

Massie smacked Latte's butt with her crop and off they went, dashing straight toward the first jump, a six-inch hurdle that Selma had never managed to clear in practice.

"Whoa!" Whitney blurted suddenly. Her black-and-white spotted horse, Oreo, flapped his ears. "She's going for it!"

Massie silenced her with a palm-lift. Latte, picking up speed, lifted his legs and soared over the hurdle. Massie held her breath and double-crossed her fingers. Jacqueline and Whitney leaned forward in their saddles. Massie squeezed her eyes shut.

"She landed it!" Jacqueline hugged her palomino, Zac Efron, around his caramel-colored neck.

Selma was still riding sidesaddle, her head and shoulders bobbling around like a rag doll on a jackhammer.

"It wasn't pretty, but she didn't fall," Whitney shouted over the crowd's applause.

"Second jump!" Massie called, as Selma went up . . . up . . . up . . . and *yes*! "Ehmagawd, she cleared it!"

Her form was awful. She was slumped to the side when she should have been leaning into the jump. But Selma was still on the horse, and that had to count for *something*.

Massie looked up at the blue, cloudless sky and winked. It was her way of apologizing to Gawd for sticking her tongue out at Him earlier. A soft breeze rustled the lush green leaves on the trees on the outskirts of the holding ring. It was His way of saying, "You're welcome."

Latte cleared the final two jumps, and Selma went along for the ride. When they were done, the crowd jumped to its feet and began chanting, "Sidesaddle, sidesaddle, sidesaddle," as she cantered toward the exit with glee.

"This is the first time in the history of the JACC we've ever seen a rider compete sidesaddle," Lill announced to the cheering crowd. "And that should bode well for her score."

The Mane Mamas raced over to the judges' table waving their arms in protest.

"Whoa!" Whitney leaned across Oreo and high-fived Massie. "You did it!"

"No," Jacqueline corrected. "*Glue* did it!"

They giggle-shimmied to the edges of their saddles and group-hugged.

"It worked!" Selma called, punching her fist in the air as she and Latte trotted through the open gate.

"Excuse me, Selma?" called the *Horse & Rider* reporter from outside the ring. "Would you mind answering a few questions? Your approach was very refreshing. Our readers would love to know what gave you the courage to try such a risky position."

Selma released the strap of her helmet and sidesaddled her way over to the lanky redhead.

Massie contemplated feeling jealous but decided against it. Let Selma have her stupid interview. It was the cover that mattered.

"Next up is Miss Whitney Bennett." Lill's voice came over the crowd again.

The girls exchanged a good-luck hand-squeeze before Whitney took off. But luck was no longer needed. Selma had come through. And if they scored like they usually did, the ribbon was theirs.

And the *Horse & Rider* cover was *hers*.

"We better help her down," Massie suggested, jumping off Brownie and racing toward Selma, who was struggling to separate her butt from the saddle.

"Is everything okay?" asked the reporter, her pencil at the ready in case the answer was no.

"Um, yeah." Selma's cheeks turned purple as she strained to lift herself off. "I'm just a little stuck."

"Must be all that popcorn you ate," Massie said quickly, trying to cover. "Salt can be so bloating. It really packs on extra weight."

"I'll push, you pull." Jacqueline stepped in the stirrup and hoisted herself up behind Selma.

"'Kay." Massie grabbed Selma's legs. "On three. Ready? One . . . two . . . three!"

Jacqueline pressed both her hands against Selma's back and shoved, while Massie grabbed her by the ankles and yanked.

Rrrrrip!

Selma toppled over in a lifeless heap, landing on Massie and knocking them both to the mud-covered ground.

Massie immediately pushed Selma off her and leapt to her feet while the medics raced toward Selma for the second time that day.

"Ahhhhh, my pants!" Selma cupped her hands over her saggy, emoticon-covered underwear and backed up against Latte for cover.

"Here they are," Jacqueline ripped a patch of oat-colored jodhpur off the saddle and waved it around like a victory flag.

The reporter began snapping pictures of Selma reaching for it as a bemused crowd gathered around them.

"What's going on here?" Lill demanded, as she forced herself past the tight circle of snickering onlookers.

Massie checked the arena. Whitney was still riding for the judges, but the audience had abandoned the bleachers and raced over to witness the sideshow.

"What happened to your pants?" Lill folded her thin arms across her flat chest and glared.

Slowly lifting her eyes in shame, Selma squinted against the bright sun, her chubby dumpling cheeks pressing up against her sparse lower lashes. "They kinda got glued to the saddle."

Lill folded back the sleeves on her crisp white button-down while she waited for a better explanation.

Massie glared at Selma, silently warning her not to confess.

"Ms. Galwaugh, are you going to tell me what happened, or would you rather explain this to your grandfather?" Lill pressed.

"Galwaugh?" Massie mouthed to Jacqueline.

Jacqueline shrugged.

"I thought your last name was Gallman," Massie couldn't help interrupting.

Dozens of other campers nodded in agreement, their velvet

riding helmets sliding forward and back. Well, *that* explained how she'd gotten into the exclusive riding camp.

"I only said that so you'd like me for *me* and not because my grandfather owns this place." Selma lowered her eyes.

"Well, that didn't work, did it?" Jacqueline blurted.

Selma's lips pursed into a puckered *O*. Her chest rose and fell in short, quick bursts, and her droopy eyes narrowed to a hate-squint. "She *made* me do it!"

Jacqueline quickly checked over her shoulder, a loose black curl whipping against her high cheekbone. "Me?"

The crowd stared at her with contempt.

Slowly, Massie backed away from the angry circle. Until . . .

"It wasn't me, it was *her*!" Jacqueline pointed at Massie. "The bottle's over there, behind the poo. Check it for prints if you want."

"Is that true?" Lill asked. "Did you dare *glue* a Galwaugh?"

Massie stared at her blankly, unsure of what to do next. Muster a fake apology to Selma? Deny, deny, deny? The answers escaped her. All she could do was stare at the redheaded *Horse & Rider* reporter and wonder what she was scribbling on her yellow legal pad.

"Well, Massie? Are you responsible for this?" Lill asked in her shaky old-lady voice.

"Nope," Massie answered with wide who-me? eyes.

Lill exhaled sharply. "Well, if an individual doesn't take responsibility, I'm going to have to disqualify the entire team for cheating."

"It's better than losing," Massie muttered under her breath.

"But I rode *sidesaddle*!" Selma stomped her foot.

"And I haven't even gone yet!" Jacqueline inched up next to Selma in solidarity.

"Well, then, will someone please tell me who did this?"

"She did!" Jacqueline and Selma shouted, their white-gloved fingers pointing straight at Massie's heart.

"You can't blame this whole thing on me!" She stared into their scorn-filled eyes. How dare they blame her for doing the only thing a true leader would do?

And then everything went quiet; the rustling leaves, the chirping birds, and even the *clip-clop* of Whitney's horse. The crowd glared at her; the staff looked disappointed, the campers shocked and disgusted. Not a single friendly palm lifted to high-five her ingenuity.

Finally, the reporter's muted snicker broke the silence. Everyone turned to face the slender redhead. "Sorry." She giggled. "But I think it's actually quite clever."

The reporter's smile widened. And Massie felt whole again.

She would get her cover after all.

"I think the glue is giving me a rash." Selma scratched her exposed bottom. "Wait until I tell my grandfather."

"There's no need for that, *is there*?" Lill quickly dabbed her powder-covered forehead with a folded yellow linen hankie.

"There will be"—Selma smirked—"if *she's* still around." She pointed at Massie again.

"Don't you wanna hear my side of the story?" Massie asked, winking at the reporter.

"Your side of the story is *over*," Lill huffed. She tucked her mousy hair behind a pointy ear. "You have one hour to gather your things." Then she turned to the reporter. "And if one word of this is printed in your magazine, I will see to it that Mr. Galwaugh takes his advertising dollars straight to *Fashionable Filly*."

The reporter click-closed her blue Bank of America pen and dropped it in her beige *Horse & Rider* canvas tote.

"Wait. . . ." Massie searched for a friendly face.

But everyone slowly backed away. Even the *Horse & Rider* reporter—the one person who'd understood her ingenuity in the face of a challenge.

She hurried toward Brownie and hoisted herself into the saddle before the pre-tears pinch behind her eyes turned into full-blown sobs of humiliation.

"I was wrong, B," She told her horse as she cued him to leave. "Losing isn't bad." She cantered past her ex-friends, leaving them behind in a cloud of dust. "It's awful."

"Wait up!" Jacqueline called from Zac Efron. "I said I was sorry!"

Massie checked her side-gloss mirror. Zac and Jacqueline were at least five stretch-limo lengths behind Brownie, galloping up the rocky trail. And Whitney and Oreo were two more behind them.

"Let's go," she muttered in Brownie's ear, then leaned forward and triple-tapped his leg. The horse picked up speed and didn't stop until they were inside the stable.

Massie jumped down, hitched her horse to the side of the wood stable, and then raced to the open barn door. She gripped it with both hands and leaned forward, using all of her weight to slide it shut. Then she kicked it with her black Hermès riding boot. Her eyes filled with tears—not because she'd scuffed the black leather, or because she'd been asked to leave Galwaugh after six years of riding excellence, but because Jacqueline and Whitney, her summer GLUs,* had betrayed her. And that hurt more than her throbbing big toe.

* GLU = Girls Like Us. Though really, only the Pretty Committee could be truly considered GLUs. Whitney and Jacqueline were hot-weather friends only, the kind that, after classes started, Massie might see once, maybe twice. They'd try to hold on with e-mails and JPEG swaps but would quickly realize it wasn't the same without horses. These girls were Forever 21 Friends—poor quality that didn't last.

"Open up!" Jacqueline banged from the other side of the heavy wooden door.

Massie dried her eyes on the velvet sleeves of her blazer. Salt was terrible for the material, but so what? The entire outfit had been exposed to friendship betrayal and was now soiled for life. It was dead to her. Just like—

"What about me?" Whitney whined. "I wasn't even *there*."

"Go away!" she called, and meant it. It wasn't like a fight with her real friends on the Pretty Committee.

"We'll make Selma call her grandfather and have him—"

"It's too late, Jacqueline." Massie unclipped the strap on her Galwaugh Girls helmet and tossed it into a murky water trough. "You're supposed to *have* my back, not stab it." Massie pressed her ear against the barn door, listening for their response.

"Forget her," Whitney's muffled voice told Jacqueline. "Let's hurry back to the cabin and get her shelves before Selma does."

Seconds later, they giggle-galloped away on their horses.

Massie faced the door, numb with disbelief. The *clip-clop*ping sounds of Oreo and Zac Efron faded and then vanished completely,

Pore-clogging dust particles hung in the light-streaked stable air, but Massie walked through it without concern. She would have plenty of time for facials now—a reality that was still sinking in. Thoughts of angry parents, summers without Galwaugh, and too much free time drifted in and out of her mind, each one competing to be the thing that drove her to tears. But she refused to give Lill or Selma or the Forever 21 GLUs that much power. Massie Block was stronger than that. Way stronger.

Until she made eye contact with Brownie.

He batted his gold-glitter lashes and sighed peacefully when she wrapped her arms around his warm neck.

Massie sniffled. "I'm so sorry I let you down." She sniffled again. He smelled like the inside of a new leather handbag. "I know you waited all winter for this. And now you're going to be stuck here, all alone, with a bunch of LBR horses. . . ."

The sob-heaves came fast and furious. Snot bubbles popped from her nose, and black mascara boogers gathered in the corners of her eyes. But Brownie just stood there patiently, allowing himself to get squeezed and snotted on while his best friend said goodbye. And that made Massie cry even harder.

She looked up at his white-blond, fur-covered face, her arms still wrapped around his regal neck. "Don't worry about me, Brownie. I'll be fine."

Brownie stomped the hay-covered ground.

"I will, I promise. Kristen is staying in, taking some lame extra-credit course at OCD over the summer, so she'll be around." Massie tried to sound upbeat so Brownie wouldn't worry. "Or I could meet up with Dylan in Hawaii or Alicia in Spain or Claire in Orlan-dull. I have a billion options."

Brownie sighed again. Only an LBR would chase after her friends during the summer, and he knew that. But Massie had to stay positive for both of them.

Just then, there was a knock on the barn door.

"Your driver is here," Lill announced from the other side of the stall. "You have exactly . . ." She paused, probably to check her wannabe-vintage, probably-fake-gold chain pocket watch. ". . . seven minutes before we escort you off the premises. Are you all packed?"

"No," Massie called, trying not to sound like she'd been crying.

"Then you'd best get a move on."

"I'd rather stay here with Brownie." She squeezed her horse a little tighter.

"What about your clothes?" Lill countered.

Massie pictured her riding wardrobe—stacks of black velvet blazers, an array of earth-toned jodhpurs, and four pairs of shiny Hermès boots. Hardly a typical summer wardrobe.

"Keep them," Massie insisted. "They smell like poo."

"Spoiled brat," Lill huffed as she crunched away, the worn heels of her old leather boots grinding against the pebbles on the trail.

"Old!" Massie whisper-barked. It was all she could manage under the circumstances.

She spent her last six minutes and forty-five seconds at Galwaugh Farms Riding Camp combing the braids out of Brownie's hair and reassuring him that she would be fine. That she would visit every chance she could. That she would hold her head high. That she would never let on how much she was going to miss this place. That she would do something *fabulous* this summer. Something alpha fabulous. Something that would show the world she was still number one.

She just had no idea what.

With thirty seconds left, Massie pulled her new iPhone from her blazer pocket and sent a quick message to Glossip Girl, notifying them of her new summer address. Then she entered her State of the Union, hoping that someday soon she and Brownie would be able to look back on all of this, toss their glossy manes over their shoulders, and giggle.

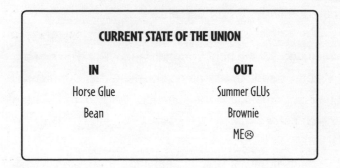

CURRENT STATE OF THE UNION

IN	OUT
Horse Glue	Summer GLUs
Bean	Brownie
	ME☹

While Isaac was wrapping up his ah-nnoyingly long lecture on the importance of good sportsmanship, Massie secretly thumb-texted the Pretty Committee.

Massie: Got the hoof from galwaugh. Put glue on Fall-a Abdul's saddle. ☺ Had no choice! Off 2 Hamptons house. Come spend the summer. Plenty of room & tons celeb parties. xox m

Seconds later her iPhone hummed.

Kristen: Sounds like a sticky situation. LOL. Can't leave W-chester till summer classes r done. Miss you!
Alicia: Hola! If the glue fits, wear it! Can't come. Just landed in Spain. Ah-mazing here! Call u l8r. I heart u!
Dylan: I always knew u were stuck up! LOL x10!!!! JK. Packing for Hawaii now. Aloha!
Claire: Come visit! Stay in r guesthouse. ☺

Massie powered down. She rested her head against the cool window and stared at maple trees as they whizzed by.

Everyone's summer plans seemed to be set, except hers. Like Selma's pathetic, lumpy butt on the saddle, she was stuck and speeding toward a situation she didn't know how to get out of.

Preparations for Kendra Block's fifth annual summer charity ball were well under way. This year's theme was "It's Easy Being Green" and was all about recycling, reusing, and reducing. Although from the look of things, Kendra had not *reduced* a thing.

Service vans with logos that read GREEN WITH ENVY PARTY PLANNERS, SIMON SWINTON'S STRING QUARTET, NATURE'S CANDY CATERING, DIVA DOG GROOMERS, GREEN THUMB FLORISTS, BORN AGAIN CRYSTAL, and JERSEY BOYS VALET filled the tree-lined driveway that led to the six-bedroom Southampton estate. The staff bustled about, setting up burlap-covered tables, perfecting all-green exotic floral center-pieces, and filling the infinity pool with floating soy candles. The grassy grounds buzzed with pre-party excitement, and Massie expected them to buzz even more now that she was home.

"Here we are." Isaac opened the back door of the family's silver Range Rover. Massie slid off the buttery tan leather seat and stepped onto the gravel driveway, her eyes fixed on the glossy white double doors of the stately mansion.

"Did you tell Mom and Dad what time I'd be home?"

Isaac looked away. His steely blue eyes were shaded by a black baseball cap, a casual accessory he allowed on sunny days to keep his balding head from burning.

A tsunami of disappointment swelled in Massie's chest. "Why aren't they waiting to greet me?"

"They must be extremely busy with the party." Isaac dabbed his beading forehead with a linen hanky, then stuffed it in the pocket of his yellow gingham Brooks Brothers dress shirt. "Everyone RSVPed 'yes' this year."

Massie lifted her tortoiseshell Diors and breathed in the salty Southampton air. "I'll be ready to dress-shop in fifteen," she told him, realizing she'd need a ground-goddess-chic ensemble for tonight's festivities.

"I'll be here." Isaac smiled like someone trying to pretend he wasn't concerned about something.

Massie turned the large brass handle on the glossy white front door and stepped inside. The black-and-white checkerboard floors were buffed to a high shine, reflecting the champagne pink chandelier overhead. The adjoining dining room contained a couple hundred tote bags, refurbished from Colombian coffee sacks. Massie couldn't help but peek inside at the swag-bag goodies:

- Bobbi Brown beach-scented candle
- Tan baby tee that read USE ME on the front and REUSE ME on the back
- Jonathan Product Dirt Texturizing Paste
- L'Occitane Lavender Harvest Foaming Bath
- Juice Beauty Blemish Clearing Serum
- Philosophy Hope in a Jar Moisturizer
- Fresh Brown Sugar Body Polish

- A card good for ten free classes at Om Yoga in South-ampton
- A raffle ticket for a trip to an eco-resort in Costa Rica (courtesy of Leo D!)

"Hullo?" she called toward the winding *Gone with the Wind* staircase. "I'm *baah-aaack*."

Suddenly, the sound of acrylic nails speed-tapping on a keyboard echoed through the foyer.

"Bean!" Massie dropped to a squat and stretched out her arms. The black pug leapt into her embrace. She smelled like a mix of Massie's dad's coconut suntan oil and her mom's sweet Cartier perfume. "I missed you soooo much!" Massie kissed the dog's forehead.

"Don't worry—we won't be bored or lonely this summer. I know a ton of people out here. And we'll probably be so busy suing Galwaugh for wrongful termination of an alpha rider we won't have time to miss anyone . . . except Brownie."

Bean hyper-licked Chanel No. 19 off Massie's neck.

Massie tossed her mint green quilted Marc Jacobs bag at the foot of the stairs, then quickly yanked off her dusty riding boots before any stable dirt could dislodge onto the cream-colored runner. Then she took a deep breath and headed up to greet her mother.

"Heyyyy." Massie beamed as she entered the airy master suite, poised to reassure her probably concerned parents that she'd bounce back from the morning's upsetting incident.

She padded past the lit gas fireplace and the gold silk duvet–covered canopy bed toward the open French doors.

Kendra, dressed in a tan Burberry tracksuit, was standing outside on her terrace. Like a queen overlooking her kingdom, she monitored the staff on the back lawn with intense concentration. "I am absolutely thrilled beyond thrilled." She petted the back of her dark brown bob.

Massie playfully rolled her eyes, knowing she was seconds away from being mother-smothered. "I thought you would be." She deposited Bean on the warm stone.

"Of course." Kendra triple-snapped her fingers at someone on the lawn and motioned for them to move whatever it was they were holding a touch more to the right. "There's nothing worse than a dripping ice sculpture. A gigantic portable freezer truck sounds perfect. *Gracias*."

"Huh?" Massie muttered before Kendra turned toward her, revealing a tiny clear headset. She lifted the mouthpiece and fixed her hazel eyes on her daughter.

Massie, not wanting to spend one more velvet-wearing second in the sun, stopped at the grapefruit pink chaise by the open French doors. "Mom, I'm okay. Please don't make a big deal about this. I'll get over it. I was thinking a lawsuit or maybe—"

"Your feelings are the *least* of my concerns right now." Kendra glared at Massie, then flip-flopped closer, her freshly pedicured toes separated by slabs of peach foam.

Gawd, what is wrong with everyone?

Kendra placed her hands on her narrow hips and sighed.

"What you did was awful. Do you realize how upset Selma's parents are?"

Massie opened her glossless mouth to respond but was instantly cut off.

"And today of all days." Kendra looked back over the balcony, then sighed angrily. "Ugh! To the left, Ronald. The *left*!"

Bean jumped down off the bed and bolted out of the room.

Kendra exhaled slowly, then continued. "Haven't you ever heard of *healthy* competition?"

"Puh-lease." Massie flopped down on the pink chaise. "*Healthy competition* is like those magazines that promise flat abs in two weeks. It doesn't exist."

"Mrs. Block." Inez's raspy voice beckoned over the small white intercom above the fireplace. "The sommelier needs his check."

"Be right there," Kendra answered, her eyes locked on Massie. "We'll finish this conversation *with* your father. Assuming he can find it in his heart to get off the golf course and help me deal with this logistical nightmare."

"Whatevs," Massie mumbled as she stood. Her mother always stressed pre-party. This was nothing new. Tomorrow they'd be getting poolside massages from that hawt Swede Puff Daddy had recommended, and all would be forgotten. "I'll be back in a few hours. I'm running out to Calypso to get a dress for tonight. Isaac is waiting—"

"You have dozens of dresses in your closet." Kendra lowered her mouthpiece and stepped back on to the balcony.

"Yeah, those would be great if this was *last* year." Massie rolled her eyes. Had her mother completely lost it? She hadn't even hugged her hello.

"Well, they'll have to do. You're grounded and are not to leave this house," Kendra snapped.

"Are you *serious*?"

"Dead!" Kendra shouted at the lawn.

"*What?*"

"Gavin, those irises are *dead*!"

"Whatevs." Massie turned on the heels of her chocolate-brown-and-periwinkle argyle socks and marched out.

She stomped into her sea foam green–tiled bathroom, tore off her stuffy riding clothes, and jammed them in the trash. *Gawd!* When had wanting to be number one become a *bad* thing? She cranked on the eucalyptus steam shower. While it heated up, she tapped on her iPhone and went straight to shopbop.com.

Her mother had said she couldn't leave the house. She'd never said she couldn't *buy* anything. Within minutes, Massie had added every item from the site's summer look book to her cart—all fifty-seven pieces. She entered her Visa number and then hit ACCEPT. Steam fogged the screen.

She wiped it clean with a lemon yellow Frette towel and—

"*Ehmagawd!*" She quickly cleaned her phone again.

But it still looked the same.

DENIED flashed in bold red letters. She tried her AmEx, her MasterCard, and even her Saks card. But DENIED kept flashing.

Camp, credit, and the cover of *Horse & Rider* magazine, all gone on the same day! Just like that.

Massie thought about crying, but her monthly tear-supply had been tapped that morning at Galwaugh. She considered pleading with Gawd for divine intervention, but He was ah-bviously still mad about earlier. She thought about running away but was suddenly too poor. The only thing she *could* do was disappear into the eucalyptus-scented steam and wait for a better idea to come along.

The Green Party was in full swing, and Massie was ready—
at last—to make her entrance, thanks to an emerald sequined
Chanel flapper dress she'd found in Kendra's long-forgotten vintage closet. Behind locked doors, she had snipped off the dangling beads and unstitched the cap sleeves. And before her mom
could say *Project Runway*, she was passing it off as last year's
Marc Jacobs. It wasn't ground-goddess chic—it was just chic.

In homage to Brownie, she'd swept her reflective dark hair
into an elegant side pony and dusted her body in iridescent
powder. If the Pretty Committee had been there, they would
have rated her a ten. Maybe even an eleven, since she'd practically made the outfit herself.

Pausing at the top of the spiral staircase, Massie peered
over the wide marble banister. Three floors below, the front
foyer was rife with East Coast millionaires and their all-too-
familiar party noises—violins screech-humming, champagne
flutes clinking, air kisses smacking, and ladies envy-shrieking
about each other's outfits.

An excited tingle fluttered behind Massie's abs. No more
hanging with hayseeds! She was at an AA party now—and
adult alphas understood her need to succeed. *They* would
support her lawsuit against Galwaugh.

"Ready to break hearts?" Massie lifted Bean and scratched the pug underneath her matching emerald silk collar, sending her hind legs into happy spasms as they began their descent.

Massie's dad, William, was standing at the foot of the staircase, looking up at her—his bald head buffed to a shine. He wore a tan linen tuxedo with a hemp bow tie. It would have seemed ridiculous if Bono hadn't worn the same one to the Emmys.

"You look beautiful, sweetheart." He took Massie's hand, escorting her down the final two steps. She kissed her dad on the cheek. His face smelled like mentholated shaving cream.

"Enjoy the party," he whispered in her Bailey Banks & Biddle diamond-studded ear, "because these are your last moments of freedom."

Massie pulled away and grinned, pretending she hadn't heard him. Her parents had never followed through on a punishment before. Why would they start now? She was practically a grown-up.

Bean let out a gentle yap. "She says you look very handsome," Massie cooed, trying to charm her easily charmed father, just in case he was serious.

"Well, Bean . . ." William smiled, giving the puppy's head a scratch. "You don't look so bad yourself." And then, just like Massie had figured, he winked and hugged her close. "It's good to have you back."

"Thanks, Daddy."

Problem solved.

"And then I said, 'Puffy or Puff Daddy, or P. Diddy, or *what-*

ever your name is, why don't you just admit it?'" Massie could hear Trini Neufeld's high-pitched voice and Gertie Shelly's snort-laugh long before her mother's two summer best friends came teetering into view. "You did nawt invent the White Party! Kendra has been hosting a color-themed party in Southampton for . . ." She put her free hand on her hip and leaned against the banister. "How many years?" She waved Massie over urgently, her shockingly orange curly bob remained surprisingly still.

"Five." Massie smiled politely, trying her hardest not to stare at Gertie, whose strapless green gown was inching its way down her Post-it-thin torso like a snake shedding its skin.

Trini took a huge gulp of fruit-filled sangria, then gripped Massie's arm. "You're just as gorgeous as ever. You simply *must* find my Ellie and say hello. She's been going on and on about hanging out with Massie Block all night." She plucked a grape out of her cocktail and deposited it on a passing tray of caramelized scallops. "You won't believe she's two years younger than you when you see the size of her chest. Poor old Roz Simmons almost popped an implant when she saw her earlier. I'm telling you, if jealousy was a penny, she'd Trump."

Gertie burst into hysterics.

"Um, where did you say she was?" Massie asked, rubbing her arm. Trini's coral talons were sharp, and Bean was starting to quiver in her presence.

"Last I saw, she was by the—"

"Great, thanks." Massie hurried away, hugging her puppy close to her chest.

Weaving through the heavily perfumed crowd toward the open French doors, Massie set off to find some Hamptons GLUs in need of a summer alpha.

The night air was humid and still. It hugged Massie's moisturized skin like a cashmere wrap. Giant leafy oaks twinkled with flickering star-shaped lights, and the thick pillars that flanked the patio were wrapped in fragrant green orchids. A dozen silver Priuses stood waiting along the circular driveway, their hired chauffeurs ready to drive tipsy guests home. Soothing sonatas played by a renowned Italian flautist drifted gently across the expansive lawn like a soft breeze.

"Massie!" A freckle-faced redheaded girl leapt out from behind a pillar. It was the ever-annoying Ellie Neufeld, her big boobs accentuated by her limeade-colored elastic-top sundress.

Massie was so startled she dropped Bean, who landed with a squeak.

"You should see the look on your *face!*" Ellie cackled, hopping from foot to foot with glee. Massie bent over to comfort Bean, but the pug tore across the lawn to her doghouse—an exact replica of the estate, only mini.

"Ellie, are you a nocturnal mammal?" Massie asked, the corners of her mouth curling in anticipation.

"No." Ellie giggled nervously.

"Then why are you badgering me?" Massie gripped her side-pony and twirled it around her finger.

"OMG, Massie!" Ellie bit her flaming-red chapped bottom lip. "Your hair is *totally* KHBC."

"Katie Holmes Before Cruise?" Massie lifted an arched eyebrow.

"Yes! You're so on it!" Ellie air-clapped.

Massie rolled her eyes and scanned the crowd for something— or some*one*—better. In the distance, atop a Balinese bed by the pool, Lindsey Kearns and Kimmi Redmond lay with their legs tangled. They were giggling at the passing waiters who, as per Kendra's request, wore nothing more than formfitting Speedos and earth-colored body paint.

Massie turned on the heel of her silver Sigerson Morrison peep-toe slides and made her way over.

"Who does your hair, anyway?" Ellie bounced along behind her, following Massie along the candlelit stone path that led to the pool. "My guy moved to Vermont to marry his life partner, even though I told him I'd need a trim before starting sixth. So now my hair is, like, homeless."

Ignoring her, Massie marched onward, swatting Ellie's words away like a malaria-carrying mosquito.

In the flickering candlelight, the green- and brown-dressed partygoers looked like swirling trees. Or was that the day's emotions catching up with her? Massie was suddenly so overcome with exhaustion she contemplated sneaking up to bed and starting fresh tomorrow. But it was too late for that now. Lindsey and Kimmi were waving her over.

"Hey." Massie stood over them, unsure whether she should commit to sitting. It was still too early to tell.

Lindsey immediately untangled herself and sat up. "Super-sweet party." The blonde's center-parted frizzy dry hair was begging for rain, and her olive Roxy halter dress and J.Crew flip-flops were daytime casual. She was in desperate need of a beauty mentor.

"Yeah, and those tiny cheesecakes are tooo cuh-yoot." Kimmi licked her wax-coated, berry-colored lips. They were the only part of her face that wasn't dotted with cheap drugstore glitter. She looked like she'd been hit in the face with a snow globe. "What are you doing back from horsey camp?"

Massie accepted a virgin piña colada from a silver waiter and took a long sip. "You mean Galwaugh *riding* camp?"

Kimmi nodded enthusiastically.

"I left."

"*Why?*" Lindsey widened her waterlogged eyes. "I heard that place was *the* best."

"It used to be." Massie straw-stirred her icy drink. "But it wasn't challenging me anymore," she lied. What business was it of theirs why she was back? They should be lip-kissing her silver-sandaled feet that she was even talking to them. "So, what are you guys up to this summer?" she asked, hovering above them.

"Surf clinic." Lindsey lifted three fingers. "Third summer in the ocean."

Hair doesn't lie.

"Can you *believe*? I think waves are, like, the scariest things ev-er." Kimmi tugged her dark girly braids, her wide brown eyes fixed on Massie, waiting for her to agree.

But Massie couldn't. Nothing was more frightening than Kimmi's second-grade style.

"I'm babysitting," Ellie proudly volunteered. She collapsed onto the bed as if raiding someone's fridge and watching cable was backbreaking work. "I already have sixty-eight dollars saved."

"Two more and you can afford a decent pedicure," Massie hissed at Ellie's unpolished toenails.

Lindsey and Kimmi cracked up. Finally! After the day she'd had, Massie was starting to feel like the only person on the planet with a functioning sense of humor.

"Move!" Massie shooed Ellie to the edge of the bed and sat.

"Are *you* working this summer?" Kimmi rolled onto her stomach and kicked her own butt with the heels of her green Marc Jacobs jellies.

"Puh-lease! I'm here to relax." Massie slammed her froth-streaked glass down on the teak pool deck. "Summer jobs are for LBRs who miss doing homework."

"*I* have a summer job." Kimmi pushed herself up.

"You mean a *jobby*, right?" Massie assumed.

"What's a jobby?" Lindsey asked with an amused grin.

"A job-hobby. Like making jewelry in your bedroom and selling it to a local boutique." Massie screwed off the top of her Blueberry Pie–flavored Glossip Girl and smeared it across her suddenly very dry lips. "Something you do for fun, *nawt* money."

"Um, no." Kimmi grabbed her recycled newspaper clutch

and stood. "I work in the SAT kiosk at the beach club . . . for *money.*"

Massie stared at her blankly.

"You know, 'Sunscreen and Towels'?"

"Oh, sorry." Massie smirked.

"It's okay." She softened. "Only in-the-know staffers call it that."

"No." Massie looked at Lindsey with a devious smile. "Sorry you *work* there."

Lindsey gasp-covered her mouth in shock.

"Glad you *don't!*" Kimmi shouted, then stormed off in a huff.

Massie sighed. "That's why I don't work. It stresses everyone out. And life was meant to be enjoyed." She lifted her palm, expecting an I-totally-agree high five from her new beta. But Lindsey left her hanging and flip-flopped away to comfort-chase Kimmi.

And that left Massie alone with Ellie, her pre-teen B-cups, and the desperate need for this miserable day to end.

Massie checked her butt in the mahogany-framed mirror by her bedroom door. "What do you think, Bean?" She rested a hand on one hip. "I found this old Diane von Furstenberg bikini in Mom's vintage closet yesterday. Thank Gawd she did the Atkins diet a few years ago. It's totally my size!"

Bean poked her pudgy head out of the just-for-show mosquito netting draped over Massie's king-size canopy bed.

"The burnt orange is unflattering *now*, but after five days of tanning I'll be ready to show it off at the beach club." She turned away from her pale, albeit toned, riding camp legs with renewed hope.

After sleeping for thirteen hours on her luxurious Duxiana mattress, Massie was starting to feel more like herself again. Her alpha battery had been recharged and her summer plan set.

Week one: Clear up credit card issues. Tan and rest poolside.

Week two: Hit the beach club. Recruit summer GLUs in need of an alpha and a good time.

Week three: Shop and spa with S-GLUs.

Week four: Yacht day trips with S-GLUs. DVD rentals and sleepovers at night.

Week five through Labor Day: Combine activities from weeks three and four.

Labor Day: Say goodbye to S-GLUs and hello to the Pretty Committee (yay x 10) September 8—Look ah-mazing for eighth grade.

It was a lot less action-packed than her schedule at riding camp. But maybe her termination from Galwaugh was a sign from Gawd, His way of telling her to take a load off and pamper herself for a change.

Someone rapped on her door. Massie reached for last year's silver-and-white sarong and wrapped it around her mother's off-limits bikini.

"You finally awake?" Kendra entered dressed in her post-party recovery outfit: lavender-scented lilac Frette robe, matching slippers filled with self-heating rejuvenation pearls, and a copper wire anti-hangover bracelet. Her face was shellacked with a potent cocktail of moisturizers reserved for those rare makeup-free days. She looked like a drawing of a woman in a coloring book, waiting to be filled in and brought to life.

"I have one question for you, Massie." Kendra folded her arms, one slippered foot tapping the beige sisal rug.

"Me first!" Massie padded over to her green apple–colored velvet chaise. Before sitting, she cranked the window open, inviting the salty ocean breeze to work its magic on her hair. "Who canceled my credit cards?"

"I did." William entered, an unlit cigar dangling from his

lips. He stuffed his thick hands in the pockets of his white boating shorts and rocked back on the heels of his Top-Siders.

"Why?" Massie stood immediately. "Are we *poor*?" she whispered.

"*You* are." William smugly flicked the brim of his navy sailor cap. "I'm not." The cap was the exact same color as his Lacoste polo and a little too matchy-matchy, but out of spite, Massie chose not to tell him.

"What's that supposed to mean?" She stomped over to the bed and flopped onto its puffy silk eiderdown, her lower lip drooping in a well-rehearsed pout.

Her parents shot each other meaningful looks. William removed the cigar. "You just got kicked out of the most prestigious riding camp in the state of New York and yet you fail to grasp the gravity of the situation."

Massie buried her face in a Jo Malone Nectarine Blossom–scented pillow and rolled her eyes. She understood the *gravity* of the situation perfectly—she was going *down*.

"What drove you to glue Maxwell Galwaugh's granddaughter to a *saddle*?" William's light brown eyes were totally twinkle-free. "What was so darn important about winning *that* race?"

Massie widened her amber eyes to heart-melting proportions. "The winning part."

Kendra sighed. "There's nothing wrong with coming in second every once in a while."

"But Daddy always says, 'Be the best Block you can be,'" Massie tried. "That's all I was doing."

"You were doing it at someone else's expense." William sat

on the edge of the bed and ducked under the mosquito netting. "And *that's* unacceptable."

"Sorry." Massie inched beside her father and put her arms around him. "Do you forgive me?"

William instantly returned the hug.

Done, done, and done.

"I won't do it again," Massie told Kendra, who was standing above them, arms folded across her sunburned chest.

"I hope not," she huffed.

"Now will you *please* turn my credit cards back on?"

"Of course, dear," Kendra purred. "As soon as you pay us back for your summer at Galwaugh."

"What?" Massie snapped. She searched her father's eyes for that just-kidding sparkle, but found all-business brown instead. "So we *are* poor!"

Her stomach filled with panic acid. Her fingertips froze. And her heart pounded a distress signal. *Poor* and *alpha* were the social equivalents of a Big Mac and a Diet Coke. Both begged the question, "Who are you kidding?"

"We are absolutely *not* poor," William insisted. "In fact, I just had a record-breaking year." He puffed out his chest with pride.

"You are going to pay us back because we want to teach you a lesson," Kendra told her daughter.

Massie stomped over to her window and looked out at the tree-lined driveway, wishing she were back at camp, free of debt, and galloping with Brownie on the lush woodsy trails. "What lesson is *that*?"

"Winning at all costs is a very bad investment." William stood. He kissed his daughter on the back of her glossy brunette head and hurried out in case she started crying.

Kendra appeared beside Massie. "Trini Neufeld was able to get you a job at the Southampton Beach Club." Her voice softened. "Ellie goes to their day camp, and they're looking for some summer help."

Massie turned to face her mother. "You *seriously* want me to get a *job*?"

"It sounds like a lot of fun," Kendra tried. "Trini says Ellie just loves the program."

A salty breeze blew by, as if trying to remind Massie exactly what she was fighting for.

"Pass!" She glared into Kendra's unwavering hazel eyes. "Mom, if I have to work this summer, I'll be too exhausted to reach my potential at school next year, and then I'll tank in the PSATs and I won't get into a good college! Really, is it worth risking everything just so Ellie can have a friend?"

"I'm afraid you don't have a choice, Massie." Kendra headed for the door. "We're not *asking* you to get a job. We're *telling* you to."

"What if I refuse?"

"*Hasta la* Visa, baby!"

Massie's stomach lurched.

The image of Kimmi sweating in the SAT hut while her friends read magazines by the pool popped into Massie's mind. It was more depressing than fur coats.

If Massie was going to do this, she needed something

glamorous. Enviable. Alpha-worthy. Something that *earned* like a job but *looked* like a hobby.

She needed a *jobby*.

"Can I at least find my *own* summer career?" Massie insisted.

Kendra pressed one shaky finger to her temple. Massie could almost see the veins bulging. "You have one week. Otherwise, I'm calling the club and telling them you accept." She shuffled toward the open door.

"Can I think about it by the pool?" Massie called.

"Whatever works." Kendra shut the door behind her, the word *works* echoing in Massie's brain like a bad J.Lo remix.

When life gave Massie lemons, she made lemon-mint spritzers. Or at least, she sipped them.

After a long, brain-numbing swig, she set the tall glass in the cup holder of the portable pedicure chair, powered off her white iPod, and wiggled her toes. It was a subtle "hurry up" hint, aimed at Rita, the famed "poolside polisher," who, after an hour, was *just* starting to apply the first coat of Chanel's Black Satin. With exactly five hours left to find a jobby before her mom forced her to work at the beach club, Massie was starting to panic.

Rita quickly lifted the tiny black brush off Massie's big toe. "Stop squirming!"

Massie rolled her eyes at the drugstore blonde's dark roots and then sighed.

"Gawd, you're so lucky."

Rita lifted her blue-colored-contact eyes. "How am *I* lucky?"

"You have a job you *love*." Massie adjusted her white Tom Ford wrap sunglasses. "Did you always dream of doing people's nails?"

"Oh yeah, sure. It's a real *dream* job." The chubby older woman clipped a stray cuticle from Massie's toe, then snickered, revealing an uneven row of top teeth.

"Well, I need to find mine." Massie checked the time on her iPhone.

"Any leads?" Rita dipped the brush in the square glass bottle.

"I don't know where to look." Massie pulled a black hardcover sketchbook and purple glitter pen from her white leather beach tote.

"Why don't you make a list of things you enjoy, and then you can think of jobs that fit those things?"

"I did," Massie opened her book and read her list to Rita.

THINGS I ♥	JOBBYS	PROS	CONS
Animals	• Vet • Dog clothing designer • Dog walker	• Save animals • A doggie fashion show would be ah-dorable • Toned legs	• Need education • Must wear lab coat • Sewing is boring • Scooping poop for a paycheck is highly un-alpha.
The Pretty Committee	Social-life planner	Comes naturally	They are away ☹
Fashion	Wardrobe Stylist	Get to shop all day . . . ☺	. . . for other people ☹
Parties	Party planner	Get paid to go to parties	Have to work while I'm at parties
Being in charge	President	Private jet	Pantsuits

"Rita?" Massie reapplied her clear Glossip Girl SPF 30 lip conditioner and peered across the lawn. The gardener was driving some tractor-style lawn mower that filled the air with the earthy smell of fresh-cut grass. It seemed like everyone was tapping into their dream job but her. "Can I ask you something?"

"Of course," Rita said, applying a second coat of Black Satin. "Anything."

Massie surveyed the list with a critical eye. "Can you grab my *Teen Vogue*? It's right next to you on my chaise. I need a break."

Rita's knees cracked when she stood.

Massie began flipping through the glossy pages. Models, leaping through the surf dressed in bikinis and long chain necklaces, mocked her with their berry-stained smiles. Toward the back there was a story about a teen girl traveling Europe and blogging on international trends. And a profile on Whitney Port, the famous intern from *The Hills*. It seemed like everyone had a glam summer jobby but her.

After a few more minutes of envy-flipping, Massie's eyes landed on a striking twentysomething with a precise jet-black bob; dark, almond-shaped eyes; and olive skin. She wore an ivory silk shift dress that had the word *be* handwritten across it in deep red lipstick. She was perched on a metallic purple Vespa, above the custom-made sidecar that carried her light gray dwarf pony, Muse.

Sometime around the holidays Massie had read about the limited-edition mini pet and tried her hardest to get one. But the dwarf-pony breeder had suggested she call back in 2011, when the waiting list opened up again.

"Listen to this." Massie wriggled her ink-colored toenails. "'Anastasia Brees, founder of Be Pretty Cosmetics, is out to make the world a more *be*-autiful place.'" Massie removed her white sunglasses. "I totally agree. I've always said ugly people should stay indoors." She started reading again. "'And in the process, this twenty-five-year-old makeup mogul has landed in *Forbes*'s Top 100.'"

Massie quickly scanned the rest of the article, devouring the stats as avidly as Isaac kept track of the Yankees. Anastasia Brees was the ultimate adult alpha. At twenty-five, she has a cosmetics empire, a private helicopter, and apartments in New York, Los Angeles, Rio, London, and Paris. She'd even placed one higher than Jessica Alba on *People*'s Most Beautiful list.

"Ehmagawd," Massie squealed. "And her favorite color is purple because it's the color of royalty. Same and same!" She ran her index finger down the page and continued reading. "'Anastasia's beauty philosophy sets her apart from all the rest. "I believe that people are most radiant when they let their inner beauty shine through," she says.'"

"Clear polish!" Massie tapped Rita's wrist with her toes. "Is it too late to switch?"

Rita sighed and reached for her glass jar of cotton balls.

The remover felt ice-cold against Massie's skin, but she barely flinched. She was too fired up. "Listen to this! Anastasia is looking for girls to be a part of her exclusive Be Pretty Cosmetics sales team!"

Massie read the details aloud, the excitement frothing up inside her like Bumble and Bumble shampoo lather. The more she read, the more enthralled she was. Each time one of the Be Pretty Cosmetics salesgirls broke the current sales record, Anastasia applied a purple streak to the high seller's hair. Flash the streak to *anyone, anywhere* in the world and it meant no wait lists necessary. No reservations required. No lines ever. It was an all-access pass to the five-star lifestyle. And it was priceless.

"I found my jobby!" She tossed her notebook on the freshly swept limestone deck.

Massie reread the article—to herself, this time—skipping the boring part about the importance of *inner* beauty. If she was going to become the top-selling Be Pretty Cosmetics girl, she didn't have time to waste on feel-good philosophies. Everyone knew that "inner beauty" was code for "good personality but not so hot on the outside."

After reading the article a third time, Massie dialed the Be Pretty Cosmetics headquarters in Manhattan.

"Be Pretty," answered a smooth female voice.

"Anastasia Brees, please," Massie blurted.

Rita giggled at the rhyme.

"I'm sorry, but Miss Brees is unavailable," the girl purred. "Can I help you?"

"I need that get-started package sent to my house priority overnight."

"I'll need a credit card to cover the shipping costs," the voice explained.

Massie reached for her bag, then stopped herself. Her entire body blushed. She kicked her foot to get Rita's attention, then mouthed, "Do you have a credit card?"

Rita shook her head no.

Massie rolled her eyes and sighed.

"Um, I don't trust FedEx. Can I pick it up?"

"Sure, we're on Spring Street in SoHo. Open till six." The receptionist hurried, as several phone lines rang in the background. "Will that be all?"

"Yup, I'll be right there."

Massie jumped off the chair and pulled the blue foam wedges out from between her toes. "Rita, I gotta find Isaac. I have a meeting in Manhattan. Can you come back tonight after dinner and finish up?"

Rita rubbed her tired eyes. "How about tomorrow?"

"I can't tomorrow. I have a jobby!" She beamed, and then waddled away on her heels. "See you at seven!"

CURRENT STATE OF THE UNION	
IN	**OUT**
Teen Vogue	*Horse & Rider*
Be Pretty Cosmetics	Be an employee at the beach club
Purple streak	Blue ribbon

Traffic was bumper-to-bumper all the way into the city. But after the five-hour round-trip, Massie and Isaac were back in Southampton, with a huge royal purple glitter–covered crate packed with beauty products, motivational CDs, and sales tips.

"What do you think?" Massie jumped out of the car and hurried across the gravel to the back of the silver Range Rover. She held a purple metallic BE PRETTY bumper sticker against the rear window, sliding it left. "Here?" she asked. Then right. "Or here?"

Isaac folded his arms across his chest. "Are you sure your mother will approve of this?"

"Puh-lease." She smoothed the sticker into place above the left taillight. "This whole job thing was *her* idea, remember?"

"It's crooked." Isaac sighed.

"And *please* unfold your arms. Otherwise no one can see your T-shirt."

He dropped his hands to his sides, revealing a purple muscle T-shirt with BE STRONG scrawled across the chest in gold glitter script. "That was the whole idea."

Massie wielded a spray tube of Be Glitzy like an eager

Saks perfume girl and misted gold sparkles all over the Range Rover. She stepped back to admire her work.

The silver SUV sparkled under the setting evening sun. It reminded Massie of Brownie and his game-day glitter. If it hadn't been for the bounty of new beauty products waiting to be unwrapped, she would have teared up at the memory.

"What have you done to *Rover*?" Kendra called from the gleaming white doorway, her hands on the waist of her cream-colored slacks.

"Mom." Massie pushed back the bell sleeves of her colorful knit Missoni wrap dress. "I'm a Be Pretty Cosmetics girl now. And all of this is part of the job—a job *you* wanted me to get, remember?" She pulled the heavy crate out of the car, hurried toward her mother, and dropped it by her fresh pedicure.

Massie sat down cross-legged in the foyer, removed her leopard-print Manolo slides, and used one kitten heel to pry open the wood flap. "You're nawt going to believe what's inside," she said, tossing handfuls of gold packing peanuts over her shoulder onto the black-and-white checkerboard floor.

"Inez!" Kendra shouted.

The Blocks' longtime housekeeper burst through the swinging kitchen door clutching a trash bag. She dropped to her bare knees and began scooping up the mess.

"Do you know how to use all of this?" Kendra tapped an acrylic fingernail against her ultra-white teeth.

"Given." Massie rolled her eyes. "I watched the instructional DVD on the ride home. But it was mostly about the company's philosophy."

"Which is . . ." Kendra lifted an opalescent glass jar of Be Young wrinkle filler and scanned the directions.

"Just a bunch of stuff about *real* beauty being on the inside and how makeup should enhance what we were born with, not try to cover it up." Massie clipped the purple satin brush holster around her hips and admired her new professional self in the round hallway mirror.

Really, she was everything a Be Pretty Cosmetics high seller should be: stylish, sophisticated, and ready to make over the world, one brassy highlight at a time. And Southampton in the summer was teeming with potential customers. Sunburned lips, dry hair, oily complexions, and last year's eye shadow were as common as crab cakes.

But not for long.

"Massie!" Ellie Neufeld appeared in the open doorway wearing an XL SOUTHAMPTON KIDZ KLUB T-shirt that fell over her bulky B-cups and skimmed her scraped knees.

"Surprise!" Trini sauntered in with a toss of her stiff orange hair. She dropped her orange Fendi on the marble credenza and spread her arms, inviting the blasting air-conditioning to cool her underarms. "Who wants to see my new Burberry—" Her wide green eyes stopped dead on the crate of makeup. "Hold. I thought Saks was tomorrow afternoon." She pouted. "Did you and Mona sneak off without me?"

"Of course not." Kendra stood and smoothed her navy silk Elie Tahari blouse. "My daughter just became a Be girl," she said proudly. "Massie, why don't you take Ellie up to your room while Trini and I visit?"

"But I have so much work to do."

"I'm sure Ellie will find your new job very fascinating."

Kendra shot her an and-that's-an-order smile. To which Massie responded with an eye roll and a foot stomp. But until she got her Visa back, Massie was a slave to her mother's infuriating demands.

"Can I help do your job?" Ellie asked as she followed Massie and her crate into her bedroom.

"How can you possibly help? Your style is worse than . . ." Massie paused, her amber eyes zeroing in on Ellie's chapped, cracked lips. Then her watery blue eyes. Then her dull complexion, her limp red hair, and her thin brows. "Of course you can help."

Massie reached into the crate and pulled out a purple makeup caddy. It was fully stocked with towers of purple boxes filled with lipstick, eye shadow, blush, gloss, and eyeliner. The she popped the Be Motivated CD into her Bang & Olufsen player and turned up the volume. It sounded New Age-y—like a female alien singing, "Be, be, be," while a pan flute whistle-moaned in the background.

"Do you want me to do your makeup?" Massie hurried to her apple green chaise by the window, where the natural light was best, and wave-invited Ellie to join her.

"Could you make me as pretty as you?" Ellie asked.

"I'm a makeup artist, nawt a plastic surgeon." Massie slid a purple satin hair band on Ellie's head, removing her orangey-red bangs from the crime scene, and took a long hard look.

She unscrewed the cap of Be Clear and squeezed a dime-size ivory dot onto the back of her hand. "I'm going to start with some foundation. It will balance out your uneven skin tone."

Ellie nodded solemnly and let Massie get to work.

"Now for some Be Rosy cheek stain to keep the morgue from hauling you away."

"Do I really look *that* pale?" Ellie touched her face.

"Stay still," Massie insisted. "And close your eyes." She brushed some smoky gray Be Sultry eye shadow on Ellie's fluttering lids. "This will totally cover those gross red veins. And this . . ." She penciled in her sparse brows with Be There brow pencil in chestnut brown. ". . . will keep you from looking like an extraterrestrial."

"Can I see now?" Ellie bobbed up and down on the chaise.

"Freeze! I still have to apply the Be Bold eyeliner." Massie rubbed the sharp tip over her wrist to check the color.

"What are you doing now?"

"Stay still." Massie tilted Ellie's head toward the light, then began lining her lids with dark blue pencil. "This will make your eyes look a lot less . . . missing."

After two coats of Be Dramatic mascara, Massie took a step back to admire her work.

"Perfect!" She beamed. "I am so good at my jobby."

"Let me see," Ellie begged.

"Almost done." Massie dusted Ellie's cheeks with translucent powder, added a touch of cheek shimmer to highlight her low cheekbones, and topped it all off with a thin coat of clear gloss over her flaming red chapped lips.

"Owwww, it stings!" Ellie whined.

"Breathe through it." Massie tossed the probably infected wand straight into the trash. "All done." She proudly handed Ellie the Be Reflective hand mirror.

Ellie grabbed it. Her blue eyes sparkled and her even skin radiated a healthy blush. She couldn't get enough of herself.

"You look good for you." Massie lifted her iPhone and snapped a picture of her first client. "I would actually be seen with you now."

"So would I!" Ellie beamed. "Thank you so much!"

"Of course, you'll need to keep this look up every day if you want to lose your LBR status."

Ellie lowered the mirror. "How do I do that?"

"Easy. Just buy the products I used."

"Then what?" She removed the headband and finger-fluffed her limp red hair.

"I'll e-mail you this 'after' picture so you can copy what I did. No charge. Just get your mother's credit card and—"

"Visa. Number four two three eight . . ." Ellie rattled off Trini's digits as if she had been reciting her own cell number. Massie quickly scrawled them down on her order pad and then calculated the total on her iPhone. "Two hundred and eighty-seven dollars," she announced, and then forwarded the number to the Be Paid address.

Done. Done. And done.

Then she lifted the mirror and checked her own reflection, trying to decide where, exactly, her purple streak should go.

"Truth is beauty." Massie lifted the sterling silver orange juice pitcher and filled her crystal glass. "At Be Pretty Cosmetics, we believe that being true to one's self *is* beautiful." She had memorized the opening speech the night before, after finding the script at the bottom of the crate. And now, after practicing it so many times, she could *almost* say it with a straight face.

"Bravo." William put down his *New York Times* and applauded. "Brains *and* beauty," he gushed while spooning a heap of muesli. "How did I get so lucky?"

"You like my outfit?" Massie stood and twirled, showing off her violet BCBG shirtdress—cinched at the waist with a pink-and-green grosgrain belt—chunky white gold bangles, and Marc Jacobs kitten-heel sandals in cobalt blue. The semi-clash of the shoes and dress boldly stated, "I'm not afraid to experiment with color," which, in her opinion, was a good message for a makeup professional to convey.

"It's a nine," William offered.

Massie's stomach lurched. "*Why?* What's wrong with it?"

Her father rubbed his bald head in confusion. "I thought you told me a nine was *great*."

"It is, but I texted my outfit to the Pretty Committee this morning, and they all gave me tens."

William shook his head and chuckled to himself. "I can't win."

"Isaac is waiting for you out front." Kendra bounced in wearing her tennis whites.

Massie pushed aside her uneaten scone, blew kisses to her parents, and retrieved the Be Polished makeup caddy from under her chair. "Come say goodbye, Bean!" she called. The pug's polished purple toenails tapped against the floor as she raced to wish Massie luck.

Outside, the sky was blue and the sun was bright—perfect for spotting people's facial flaws.

"Ready?" Isaac called as he wiped glitter off the Range Rover windshield.

Massie lifted her purple caddy to show that she was. He opened the door and she slid onto the tan leather.

"So where are we headed?" Isaac asked, adjusting the rearview mirror after he climbed into the driver's seat.

It didn't take Massie long to remember Frizzy Lindsey from the Green Party.

"Foster Crossing. The Kearns estate." Massie leaned forward and popped *her* version of a Be Inspired CD into the car's player and stabbed at the buttons—enough of the pan-flute-alien music. She leaned back in her seat and began tapping her kitten heels to Fergie's "Glamorous."

"Flying first class, up in the sky . . ." Massie sang along, cranking up the volume and ignoring Isaac's pained expression. *"Poppin' champagne, living my life in the fast lane . . ."*

Isaac lowered the music.

"By the way . . ." Massie leaned forward, breathing in his minty aftershave. ". . . where's your BE STRONG shirt?"

"What?" Isaac cranked up the volume. "I can't hear you!"

Massie giggled, staring out the window at neat rows of grapevines and occasional glimpses of ocean. American flags blew from gray-shingled beach estates, and vintage Mercedes sat parked on their crushed shell driveways.

They pulled onto Foster Crossing and drove past the No SOLICITORS sign. Then straight up the Kearns's long—but not as long as the Blocks'—tree-lined driveway.

The long ranch house was made entirely of floor-to-ceiling windows. A wall of nine-foot manicured hedges surrounded their vast property to keep potential stalkers from seeing inside, but once you passed those, it felt like the Kearns were on display at some sort of futuristic people-zoo.

Isaac parked behind a hunter green Jaguar. Massie smoothed out her Theory shirtdress and grabbed her purple caddy.

"Wish me luck!" Massie skip-shuffled up the bluestone pathway and arrived at the smoky glass doors. She pressed the intercom button and announced herself.

Frizzy Lindsey answered wearing an athletic light blue tankini top and lace-front board shorts with a dizzying Hawaiian print. She'd wrestled her brittle blond hair into a frayed topknot and had stuck a soy sauce–stained wooden chopstick in it.

"Hey, Frizzy." Massie flashed her best Be Glossy grin.

"It's *Lindsey*," she snapped, her bloodshot green eyes narrowing to a hateful squint.

Massie cleared her throat and began reciting the script.

"Truth is beauty. At Be Pretty Cosmetics, we believe that being true to one's self *is* beautiful. Let Be Pretty Cosmetics help you find the woman you were meant—"

Frizzy Lindsey held her ocean-pruned palm up to Massie's face. "Are you trying to *sell* me something?" A vindictive smile formed at the corners of Lindsey's zinc-streaked lips. "What is this, like, a summer job?"

Massie clenched her fists, determined to stay professional. "Inner beauty is more important than outer beauty," Massie told her, but the words tasted wrong in her mouth, like a latte made with whole milk and real sugar.

She pushed past Lindsey and entered the ultra-modern sun-drenched home. If she could just find a place to set up, the products would speak for themselves. She spotted a white plastic coffee table in the living room and hurried toward it. "At Be Pretty Cosmetics, we're not trying to cover you up with abrasive, animal-tested products. Quite the opposite. We want the world to discover the real you—"

"Enuff, dude." Lindsey flip-flopped across the espresso-colored wood floors, following Massie into the living room. "What about all that stuff you said? You know, like how summer jobs are for *losers*?"

"Um, first of all," Massie said, flicking open her makeup caddy, "I'm *nawt* a *dude*. And second of all, I'm *nawt* trying to sell you something. I'm just trying to help you discover your inner beauty." She swallowed hard.

"The sign out front says No Solicitors." Lindsey smirked.

Massie's stomach lurched. More than anything, she wanted to barf a mouthful of insults all over the surfer's peeling skin. But the training DVD devoted three whole minutes to leaving a "no go" with grace. So she held back. For Anastasia.

"In that case"—Massie closed her caddy and headed for the door—"thanks for your time, and enjoy your beauty."

Without another word, Massie smiled, turned on her blue kitten heel, and tried hard to walk, not run, back to the Range Rover.

"Any luck?" Isaac asked gently as Massie slammed the passenger door.

"The Riordan-Buccolas' on Murray Lane," Massie told him as she crossed Lindsey's name off her Be Home visit log with purple eyeliner.

Kelsey Riordan-Buccola was related to either Dolce or Gabbana through her mother's third marriage to a Sicilian exporter. But her real father must have been a total wannabe, because Kelsey's blood type was LBR positive. Unfortunately, all the couture in the world couldn't make up for Kelsey's patchy skin, close-set eyes, and unibrow. However, a Be Pretty transfusion and some tips from a seasoned alpha *could*.

They were greeted at the gate by a security guard who patrolled the grounds in a bulletproof golf cart. Once cleared for entry, they drove down the Riordan-Buccolas' half-mile-long driveway and parked beside an angel fountain that peed moldy water.

"Truth is beauty," Massie repeated to herself, hoping that

at some point the feel-good philosophy would actually start to make sense. Because come awn, since when had *truth* ever landed anyone a modeling contract?

"*Be* good." Isaac smiled as he opened her door.

Massie tightened the grosgrain belt on her shirtdress, gripped her case, and climbed the slate steps to the Riordan-Buccolas' front door.

The enormous gray stone manor was more Hogwarts than Hamptons, but Massie silenced her inner critic. Anastasia had earned her place on the Most Beautiful People list by finding the beauty in people with bad taste and worse skin, and so would she.

Ding, dong, ding, dong . . .

The doorbell sounded like the Riordan-Buccolas had hired the New York Philharmonic to play every time someone came to visit. Massie looked around, half expecting to see the orchestra camouflaged in the rosebushes.

. . . ding, dong, ding, dong . . .

A shiny-haired brunette around Massie's age, wearing an impossible-to-get beige Stella McCartney slip dress, opened the castlelike door. The girl had the Riordan-Buccolas' signature ski-slope nose but otherwise she looked wholly unfamiliar. Maybe Kelsey's stepcousins from the old country were visiting?

"Is Kelsey Riordan—"

. . . ding . . .

Massie tried again. "Is Kelsey—"

. . . dong . . . ding . . .

Massie threw her hands on her hips and waited.

. . . dong.

"Okay, *now* it's done." The girl grinned. "Massie? Is that you?" She flashed an even-toothed smile.

"Ehmagawd, *Kelsey*?" Massie looked deep into the girl's sapphire blue eyes. "You look ah-mazing."

Kelsey smiled appreciatively. "Thanks."

Speechless, Massie shook her head in disbelief while she awe-admired Kelsey's stunning metamorphosis. Her expertly placed chestnut highlights framed her suddenly flawless skin, and the neutral-colored slip dress made her tan pop. "I hardly recognized you without the—"

Pimples? Braces? Hairy man-legs?

"Glasses," Kelsey finished with a knowing smile. "Lasik eye surgery. Now I can actually see the price tags on this season's wardrobe. Not that they matter, of course." She stepped outside and sat on the wide slate steps.

Kelsey shielded her blue eyes from the afternoon sun and peered at Massie. "So, what are you doing here? Did Becki Rogan blab about the boxes I just got from D&G? Because I am so not opening them until my birthday, which isn't till July."

"Puh-lease." Massie tried not to sound insulted as she took a seat next to the new-and-obviously-surgically-improved Kelsey. But come awn! Even if her credit cards were canceled for the next ten years she wouldn't act all envy-impressed by Kelsey's connections. At least not in public. "I came to show you some *ah*-mazing new beauty products I discovered."

Massie popped open her makeup caddy and leaned back so as not to cast a shadow on her treasure.

Kelsey quickly turned to shoo a yellow butterfly that had begun fluttering around her glistening hair.

"At Be Pretty Cosmetics," Massie started, "we believe that truth is beauty."

Kelsey was still shooing, so Massie fast-forwarded to the end of her speech. "Let Be Pretty Cosmetics help you become the woman you were meant to *be*."

"I agree," Kelsey said, satisfied that the butterfly was gone. She tucked her glossy hair behind one ear to reveal the same Harry Winston chandelier earrings Massie had gotten for Christmas. Only Kelsey's were bigger. Massie decided she loathed the girl more than she had loathed last year's leg-warmers-and-heels trend. "But I only use Nars and Stila." She gave Massie's purple caddy a dismissive glance.

"But Be Pretty products are—"

"Sorry, Massie," Kelsey interrupted, her smile patronizing. "Ever since I heard that Sienna Miller only uses Nars foundation, I swore I'd never use anything else. And now everyone tells me I look like her. In fact," she said, peering at Massie, "you could probably use a little yourself. Your cheeks are starting to look a little ruddy."

Massie stared at Kelsey, her mouth agape. Six months ago, Kelsey Riordan-Buccola had probably had her eye sockets surgically removed from the sides of her nose and had holed up in her family's tacky faux-castle to recover. Who was *she* to—

The red Samsung in Kelsey's hand started playing Kanye

West's "Stronger" and she waved it at Massie. "Gotta take this." She stood and hurried inside. "Good luck, you," she shouted just before closing the carved wood door in Massie's face.

Who did Kelsey Riordan-Buccola think she was? Her beauty was new—just like her money.

Massie stomped down the stairs, scraping the tacky imported slate with every grinding step. Nobody tossed Massie Block out like last season's It bag.

Nobody.

Lindsey Kearns and Kelsey Riordan-Buccola were going to *be* sorry.

The warm onshore breeze did things to Massie's naturally wavy hair that Galwaugh's dry forest gusts could only dream of. It added curl and bounce and a flirty playfulness that said, "Lip-kissed by nature and loving it." But secretly, Massie would have given anything to be back at horse camp. There, she was a winner. But here, the whole *jobby* thing was making her feel like a total L—

Massie shook the thought from her head. It was a new day. There was still hope.

On the back patio, she set her tiny cappuccino cup down on the marble-and-wrought-iron table with a clink. She pushed her dark Ferragamo sunglasses up her nose, unfolded a laminated map of Southampton, and examined it like a general planning the invasion of a small, wealthy country.

"This is serious, Bean."

The pug paced at Massie bare feet.

"Yesterday was a disaster." Massie sharpened a Be Defined lip pencil, releasing eggplant purple shavings into the bright, salt-scented air. She drew *X*'s over Frizzy Lindsey's and Kelsey's streets. "So we're going to have to try another tactic." She circled Herrick Road, where the less-fortunate year-rounders lived.

Bean let out an anxiety sneeze.

"I know! But it's our only chance." Hopes of her purple streak were disappearing faster than marked-down Zac Posen at a Barneys sale. "No one loves inner beauty more than unattractive wannabes. They'll be all over this stuff."

Massie scooped Bean up with renewed determination. Nothing made her feel more streakworthy than her mother's vintage Pucci halter dress, which she'd paired with white skinny Citizens, emerald green Tory Burch flats, and wood bangles from Calypso. Massie knew one thing: If she could pull off skinny white jeans, she could pull off anything.

"Isaac!" she called, heading for the driveway. "To the year-rounders on Herrick Road!"

"Are you sure about this?" Isaac turned onto Herrick Road and parked the Range Rover in front of the first house on the street.

"Ew." Massie peered over her sunglasses at the small, cottage-style house with pink flowered curtains in the window. A green flag with appliquéd flowers hung from a pole above the screen door. If the décor was any indication, whoever lived here was in desperate need of guidance.

She tiptoed to the front door to avoid catching her heel in the weed-infested cracks in the pavement. The potted geraniums on either side of the porch were wilting in the heat. And Massie knew exactly how they felt. She pinched the brass knocker, pulled it back, and dropped it as if it were made of rayon.

"Yeah?" A girl Massie's age dressed in an oversize New York Knicks basketball jersey opened up and peered suspiciously at the Range Rover. Her burgundy-from-a-box shoulder-length hair was stringy, and her poo-brown eyes bulged more than Bean's. Massie was grateful she was wearing her dark Ferragamos, because the girl's unsightly smattering of upper-lip hair was making Massie's eyes water.

"Beauty is truth," Massie began, rattling off the speech with ease. "At Be Pretty Cosmetics—"

"Who's there, Cora?" a woman called, then coughed violently.

"Just some girl selling makeup," the girl shouted back.

Just some girl!?

Massie parted her hairless lips, preparing to point out that she was special and superior and far from just some *anyone* when the woman yelled, "Tell her we're an Avon family and come finish cleaning up this puzzle."

Cora shrugged like there was nothing more she could do. Without another word she gave the screen a push and padded down the narrow pea green–carpeted hall. Massie stood there in shock as the door slowly wobbled its way shut.

She looked down at her flawless outfit, just to make sure she wasn't wearing her Cosabella boy shorts on the outside of her skinny jeans, which she wasn't. So what, then? Were people threatened by her trendsetting style? Her timeless beauty? Her unstoppable alpha energy? Whatever it was, Massie was determined to turn her luck around. If she didn't, she'd never see her pride—or her poor Visa—again.

Massie collapsed onto the navy-and-cream Italian silk sofa in the Blocks' guests-only living room. She slipped off her Tory Burch flats and twirled her platinum necklace around her index finger until her finger looked white and strangled. "This must be how Isabella Rossellini felt when she got dumped by Lancôme."

Bean took a running leap and landed on the matching ottoman. She nudged the latest copy of *Vogue* toward Massie with her wet nose.

"No, thanks." Massie turned away. Not even seven hundred pages of bored and hungry models could cheer her up. Bean whimpered and collapsed in a ball on top of *US Weekly*, covering Rumer Willis's ample head.

Just two days ago, Massie's future had been bright. Bright purple, to be exact. She'd imagined leading the Pretty Committee into every three-star Michelin-rated restaurant in Manhattan, with the latest impossible-to-get bag by MJ, Prada, or Gucci slung over her tanned shoulder. One flash of her purple streak and the hostess would instantly show Massie to the best table, even if it meant asking some It chick to leave. Now things looked very different.

"Massie Block!"

Bean sprang off the guests-only ottoman at the sound of Kendra's voice echoing through the foyer.

"I'm in here!" Massie stood and quickly smoothed the crater in the down pillow before it ratted her out for sitting on it.

Kendra pushed open the French doors and *click-clack*ed across the hardwood floors. She stopped in front of Massie and placed both hands on the waist of her camel Escada Sport stretch pants. A rose-colored Bottega Veneta tote dangled from one wrist, a Bliss Spa bag from the other. She looked like a mannequin in the window at Saks.

"What is it?" Massie sighed. Bean cowered behind her legs, peeking out every few seconds.

"I just spent the afternoon with Trini Neufeld," Kendra said angrily, as if there was a bigger point to the story than just that. "And it seems as though—" She paused and tilted her head to the right, sensing the slight dent in one of the couch pillows. "Massie, what in the world possessed you to transform Ellie Neufeld into a Paris Hilton and then *charge* her for it?"

"Whadaya mean?" Massie asked innocently. She slid her Tory Burch flats back onto her Be Smooth–moisturized feet, preparing to make a run for it.

"That's not going to work this time." Kendra glowered at her. "Trini Neufeld is absolutely furious, and after the incident at the club—"

"What happened?"

"Trini was mingling at brunch this morning when Ellie,

along with five of her little friends, sauntered by wearing Trini's stilettos, gray eye shadow, and red lipstick, shouting, 'Be brash,' at everyone they passed."

Lip stain, Massie thought. Nawt *lipstick*.

"Why would you sell a ten-year-old girl three hundred dollars' worth of makeup?"

"Have you *seen* her?"

"She's *ten*!" Kendra shook her shopping bags in frustration.

But Massie didn't defend herself. Not when her Visa was at stake. Instead, she dug her nails into her clammy palm and silently begged her mouth to stay out of it.

"Your job is to be a *makeup* artist, not a *con* artist." Kendra squinted in disappointment. "Taking advantage of friends is completely unacceptable."

Massie lowered her amber eyes, the way someone who felt bad would do. But how could she *really* feel bad when she'd saved Ellie from drowning in LBR quicksand? The girl obviously felt more confident or she wouldn't have been *Be-ing Brash* at brunch.

Massie thought back to the afternoon of her one—and only—Be Pretty sale. Ellie had been a prematurely B-cupped caterpillar until Massie's alpha instincts and good old-fashioned honesty turned her into a butterfly. And she'd done it without that corn-dog script from Be Pretty Cosmetics. In the words of Anastasia Brees, beauty *is* truth.

And then, for some reason, that phrase repeated itself over and over in her head, like the chorus of a song you just can't seem to shake. *Beauty* is *truth*. . . . *Beauty* is *truth*. . . . *Beauty* is *truth*. . . .

Ehmagawd! Beauty is truth!

It was so obvious. All she had to do was tell her clients how sincerely ugly they were and they'd load up on product. Just like Ellie had. And then the silver card and the purple streak would both be hers.

Done, done, and done.

This time, when Frizzy Lindsey opened the smoky glass doors, Massie was ready.

"One question. Do you want to hang ten or *be* a ten?" She pushed past the surfer girl and marched straight into the stark-white, kitschy plastic furniture–filled home.

"Huh?" Lindsey dried her hay-hair with a bleach-spotted green towel.

"Where's your bedroom?" Massie gripped her purple make-up caddy with both hands and rocked back and forth on the heels of her red Prada wedge sandals.

Lindsey pointed down a blue-lighted corridor. Extra-long aquariums filled with exotic fish had been built into the stucco walls, reflecting rippling water onto the ceiling.

"Great. Let's go." Massie led the way, trying not to make eye contact with a creepy pink squid that followed her down the length of the hallway.

Barefoot, Lindsey follow-chased her. "What do you think you're doing?"

Massie stopped in front of a tank filled with bumpy star-fish.

"The same thing a clean mirror and some natural light would do if you let them."

"And what's *that*?" Lindsey pushed the sleeves of her light blue GOT SURF baby tee over her peeling shoulders. She rubbed off a layer of skin and released it, letting it drift to the espresso-stained floor.

"I'm going to tell you exactly what I see."

Massie let herself into what she assumed was Lindsey's bedroom. Glossy posters of surfers charging cobalt blue waves covered every inch of wall space. Her canopy bed frame was built from shellacked wooden longboards, and strings of brown-and-white pukka shells surrounded it like a curtain. It was to the rest of the sleek, modern house as Lindsey's hair would be at a Pantene convention—frighteningly out of place.

Massie set her caddy down on a pink corduroy beanbag and slumped below the porthole-shaped window. She triple-tapped it, inviting Lindsey to cross the room and join her.

When she did, Massie circled her twice, making mental notes.

"*What?*" Lindsey released her green towel to a Mexican blanket turned rug.

"The ocean has given you a major case of high-and-dry."

"What's that?" Lindsey sat. The beans rustled and sank under her fit body.

"Surfing has toned you. Your butt is nice and *high*. But everything above it is d-r-y." Massie handed Lindsey the purple Be Reflective mirror and eyed her blue-and-black board shorts with contempt. "I'm sure I speak for everyone on Long Island when I say I'd like to see less coverage on the bottom and *ah* lot more on top. Starting with your face."

"Seriously?" Lindsey touched her scaly cheek like some post-op patient who'd just removed the bandages. "Is that why I'm always itchy?"

"And blotchy and uneven and often called Lizard Kearns behind your back? Yes."

Lindsey stood. "What should I do?"

"For starters, how about a pair of bikini bottoms."

Massie pulled several purple boxes from her caddy. One by one, she laid them out on a low bamboo magazine table. "When you start wearing bikinis, everyone will realize you're a girl. And if you *look* like a girl, you should *feel* like a girl, right?"

Lindsey blinked her bloodshot eyes in agreement.

"So allow me to introduce Be Supple all-over body whip, Be Flawless foundation, and Be Silky conditioner. Oh, and let's not forget Be Slick hot-oil treatment, which you need to apply to your scalp aysap." Massie held up her hand and rubbed her fingers against her thumb. "Your hair is seriously sucking the moisture of this room. You should consider a humidifier until the conditioner kicks in. I'm finding it hard to breathe."

"But I was planning on surfing later." Lindsey scratched her sunburned forehead.

"Were you also planning on filing your nails with your lips? Because they are about as smooth as an emery board."

"Wait! I know what you're doing," Lindsey narrowed her already-narrow green eyes. "You're trying to make me feel bad about myself so I'll buy your stuff."

"No, I'm trying to make you feel bad about yourself so you

stop looking *bad*. You are under absolutely no obligation to buy." Massie handed her a tube of Be Slick. "Just try it. Wet your hair, rub it in, and rinse it out after five minutes. I'll take it from there."

Lindsey lifted her green towel off the floor and padded off to the bathroom. She returned shortly, with comb tracks in her blond hair and a smile. "Not a single tangle!"

"I told you." Massie beamed. It felt good to put herself aside for a minute to help the less fortunate. Finally, she understood her mother's addiction to charity parties.

"What else can you do?" Lindsey love-patted her wet hair.

"Hmmmm . . ." Massie folded her arms across her mother's vintage red-and-orange Pucci shift dress. "I assume you like the natural look, so I'd like to keep it simple. Tinted moisturizer for extreme flakiness, cheek stain, under-eye cream, lid concealer, a palate of neutral shadows, blue eyeliner to reduce redness, brown waterproof mascara, cheekbone highlighter, lip exfoliator, lip quencher, lip gloss, brow remover, brow rebuilder, and rose-scented face mist to counteract the fishy smell of the ocean."

"Do you have anything to make my lips look fuller?"

"How full? Garner full or Johansson full?"

"Johansson."

"How much time do you have?" Massie raised one perfectly plucked eyebrow.

"Well, since I'm not surfing today . . ." Lindsey peeked at her hula-girl wall clock. "Until bedtime."

A few hours later, Massie could hardly recognize the girl

in front of her. Lindsey's sparkling green eyes shimmered. Her skin glowed in all the right places and, with the help of various blushes and brushes, her cheekbones had emerged from hiding. The wild frizz had been tamed into glossy blond tendrils that bounced just above her shoulders and framed her now-pretty face.

"Can I look?" Lindsey squirmed under Massie's translucent powder brush.

"Almost." She gave Lindsey's nose a final tap.

"Now?" Lindsey bobbed up and down on the beanbag.

"Now." Massie handed off the Be Reflective mirror with pride. "You look so good for you."

Lindsey gasped. "How can ever I repay you?"

"Visa works." Massie grinned.

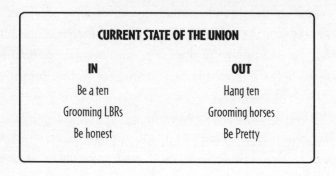

CURRENT STATE OF THE UNION

IN	OUT
Be a ten	Hang ten
Grooming LBRs	Grooming horses
Be honest	Be Pretty

Word spread quickly after Massie rehabilitated Lindsey's face with her unique "Truth Is Beauty" philosophy. For the last three days, Massie had been pounding the pavement like a pair of clunky Ecco clogs, giving free physical evaluations, drying tears, and selling thousands of dollars' worth of Be Pretty Cosmetics.

Encouraging "congratulations" and "keep up the good work" e-mails from the company flooded Massie's inbox. And promises that she was on Anastasia's radar fueled her drive. But purple streak aside, the last seventy-two hours were starting to take their toll. Dark circles had formed on the tender tissue beneath her eyes, and her hair was losing its luster. Her lips were dry from hours of fake smiling, and her tweezing hand was starting to cramp. It was time to fast-track her sales, cash out, and retire early.

Her solution had been to invite every girl between the ages of twelve and sixteen—with authorization to sign her parents' Visa—to a Be Made Over party. And all thirty-eight of them had showed.

They mingled on the elegant lawn, drinking antioxidant-rich Bossa Nova açai drinks and nibbling on sushi-grade salmon rolls packed with skin-beautifying Omega 3s. Waiters in purple lab coats offered complimentary straw hats to keep the sun from burning the girls' product-free faces. Star-shaped Be a Star mirrors hung off the branches of the big oak. Five lavender satin–covered tables were packed with products that had been overnighted from the SoHo office. But no one dared purchase a thing until she had her free consultation with the hostess.

Massie, feeling confident in a lime green silk Marc Jacobs dress and silver woven Tory Burch wedges, sat in the leather wing chair in the center of the lawn. All the guests were wearing Be Pretty name tags that spelled out their names in purple glitter. Except Massie. Everyone already knew who she was.

She applied a final coat of Be Nude peach gloss—her Piña Colada Glossip Girl was safely hidden away until the customers cleared out—lifted her legs onto the matching ottoman, and crossed her ankles. It was time. "Line up, ladies!"

Instantly, the girls raced over and arranged themselves single file as if visiting Santa at the mall.

"Welcome to the Be Made Over party." Massie smiled humbly while everyone applauded. "One by one, you will approach the chair so I can analyze your face. I will give you instant feedback and tell you what products to buy. Everything you need to look *Be*-yoo-tiful is on one of those tables behind me. Grab what you need, and Isaac will check you out."

The driver, decked out in a purple lab coat and dark Versace sunglasses, smirk-waved from behind a white Mac PowerBook.

"Let me remind you, this is not for the thin-skinned." Massie took off her white MJ push-lock sunglasses and replaced them with a pair of sophisticated antique silver Chanel frames from her mother's vintage closet. The prescription-free lenses gave the illusion that she could detect all flaws, no matter how tiny. "Prepare yourselves," she said to the eager faces staring back at her. "I am going to be brutally honest, because truth *is* beauty. So if you're not ready to hear what I see, help yourself to a complimentary sample packet and go home to your mommy. No hard feelings."

Girls began biting their brittle nails, twirling their dry hair, and lowering their undefined eyes. But no one left.

"Okay, is everyone ready?"

Just then, a low-flying helicopter circled overhead, kicking up a wind that blew the tree mirrors and made them clang like a stack of bangles. The girls gazed up at the blue sky and clutched their straw hats. The helicopter swooped toward the ocean, and the girls shrugged off the interruption. It was probably just the Seinfelds.

"Let's get started," Massie said to the first girl in line, and checked the name tag stuck to her multicolored polka dot–infested tank. It said BE MARIN. "Hi, Marin." She removed her legs from the ottoman, inviting the girl to sit.

"Hi." Marin blushed. "Thank you so much for—"

Massie lifted her palm. "I need total concentration," she insisted as she leaned forward and analyzed the strawberry-hued thirteen-year-old. The girls were silent, probably anxious to know if the rumors about Massie's tough-love sales technique were true.

"I feel a little nauseous." Massie covered her mouth and leaned back in the white leather chair.

Marin offered a sip of her of Bossa Nova.

"Drinking won't help." Massie quickly recovered. "But a good foundation will."

"Huh?" Marin crinkled her freckle-covered nose.

"I see dots on your face and dots on your shirt, and the whole thing together is making me dizzy. You need some Be Flawless to even out your complexion. You also suffer from a bad case of newborn-gerbil eyes. I recommend Be Bold mascara to bring out your lashes, unless of course you *want* to look like Richard Gere." She scribbled something on her Claire Fontaine graph-paper pad, tore off the top sheet, and handed it to her first customer. "Enjoy your beauty. Next."

Marin lowered her head and hurried over to the products table before anyone could tell if she was crying or not.

Be Cathie sat next, and in the interest of time, Massie got right down to business.

"Blackheads *and* whiteheads? Gawd, I am so sorry."

Cathie cupped her swollen nose.

"It looks like someone threw salt and pepper at your face." Massie handed her a sheet of paper. "Get Be Clear face wash and the entire Be Clear line. I'm talking exfoliator, toner, foundation, concealer, and blush. It's noncomedogenic, so it won't clog your.pores. But before you use it, see Porsha for an extraction facial and Dr. Miller for a nose job. Their numbers are on the back. Enjoy your beauty. Next!"

A ghostly pale girl named Angelica sat down.

"Be Rosy and Be Bronze. Aysap." Massie handed her a sheet of paper. "And check the family history for anemia. Your see-through skin tells me you're low on iron. Eat a steak. Enjoy your beauty. Next!"

A girl covered in makeup hurried onto the ottoman. Her lids were heavy with green shadow, her brown eyes lined with blue, her cheeks caked with terra-cotta blush, and her lips stained cherry red.

Massie peeked at her name tag, then back up at her brought-to-you-by-Crayola face.

"Um, Noelle, did you get trapped in Sephora during an earthquake?"

Everyone in line giggled except Noelle, who simply shook her head no as she tooth-scraped the waxy color off her bottom lip.

"You need a complete make-*under*," Massie insisted. "Go get four bottles of Be Clean makeup remover and then everything marked Be Natural. When I'm done here, I'll be glad to show you how to apply it. Hurry! Before someone accuses you of binge-eating melted M&M's. Enjoy your beauty. Next!"

"Hey there." Kimmi Redmond smirked, her overly glitter-dusted face winking flecks of light at anyone who dared look at her head-on. "Enjoying your *job*?"

"It's nawl a job—it's a *jobby*," Massie insisted, just as the helicopter returned. The low rumble of the whirling blades reverberated in her chest. "Probably an *US Weekly* photographer!" she shouted over the deafening noise.

The girls nodded in agreement as the helicopter circled

the estate with undeniable interest. Hats and napkins blew across the pristine lawn. Massie noticed her parents standing on the back patio.

At first she assumed they were concerned by the high-flying intrusion, but she quickly changed her mind. They weren't looking up at the sky or chasing after windswept debris— they were lovingly watching their daughter outperform any other Be Pretty Cosmetics sales rep in the company's six-year history. And that was *almost* better than a limitless Visa and an all-access hair streak.

Almost.

Finally, the helicopter tilted left, scattering iridescent flecks into the air. As quickly as it had come, it zipped away, leaving a purple sparkle–covered lawn in its wake.

Giggle-gasping, the girls shook out their hair and brushed off their outfits.

"Kimmi!" Massie said to her glitter-covered lap, "this is why you have to tone it down. One gust and we're *all* living in a snow globe."

"It wasn't *me*," Kimmi insisted, her blue eyes wide with innocence.

Massie glared at Kimmi, silently accusing her of lying. Until she realized . . . Kimmi abused gold, silver, and pink glitter.

Not purple.

Massie's heart soared. Without another word she removed her fake-prescription glasses and lifted her eyes. The sky was empty and silent. But if her alpha instincts were right, it wouldn't stay that way for long.

Massie felt like her iPod Classic—low on power and white.

The makeover party had been a major hit, but she was beyond exhausted and extremely tan-deprived thanks to her hectic jobby. An afternoon lounging on a water-resistant ivory chenille chaise and cooling off in the rose petal–infused infinity pool was exactly what she needed. There would be plenty of time to tabulate her sales when the sun went down. Not that she needed a calculator to know she'd broken every sales record in Be Pretty Cosmetics history. The countless follow-up text messages from her thirty-eight satisfied customers were proof enough.

Compared to the morning, the Block estate grounds were remarkably silent. The staff was on lunch break, William was playing golf, and Kendra was power-walking to town to buy Massie's favorite low-fat crab cakes—a well-deserved treat for her hardworking daughter. The only sounds came from the tweeting birds, the neighbor's humming lawn mower, and the waves lapping against the caramel-colored sand in the distance. Even Bean, who usually snored, was breathing easy next to Massie's Be Soft–exfoliated feet.

She was about to text the Pretty Committee with an update on the day's events when the whirring sound returned.

Bean scampered up the chaise and burrowed into Massie's wavy summer hair.

"Yes!" Massie sat up and hugged Bean a little too hard. She lowered her white-framed MJ sunglasses, slipped on her mother's black-and-white Chanel sarong, and thanked Gawd she was wearing the matching black bikini with the gold *C*'s at the cleavage.

The chopper was visible in the distance. It looked like the tadpole-shaped birthmark on the cheek of new customer number sixteen, Jenny Browning. Bean leapt off the lounge chair and darted nervously around the bluestone pool deck, barking at the sky.

The shimmering tadpole got bigger and the dicing propellers grew louder. "It's back!" Massie shouted at the helicopter, her heart beating venti triple-shot Frappuccino style.

Massie immediately sat up and tossed her Glossip Girl SPF 30 into a rosebush.

Her skin cooled in the dark shadow of the Hamptons Bird as it descended. The grass blew flat. The pool water rippled. And the rose petals lifted into the air and swirled up like snow in reverse. Golden highlights whipped against her sun-kissed cheeks, and purple glitter rained down from the heavens for the second time that day.

The lack of a landing pad was of no concern to the pilot as the helicopter wobble-descended, then rested its silver blades in the middle of the lawn.

"Ehmagawd," Massie mouthed into the wind. The words *Be*

Pretty were scrawled across the bronze door in purple glitter script.

Only one person could be inside.

Massie scooped up her trembling puppy and hurried to greet her VIG (Very Important Guest).

The door opened and Anastasia Brees lifted goggles and a gold helmet off her head. With a single shake, her precise black bob fell right into place. She wore a breezy lavender draped-over-the-shoulder goddess gown, which could have passed for neon against her deep olive skin. It made Massie completely rethink her Juicy-sweats-when-flying rule.

The makeup mogul emerged barefoot, clutching her light gray dwarf pony, Muse. Her cotton-white mane and mini hoofs made Massie's fingertips tingle. She wanted to grab the ah-dorable little thing, smother her in kisses, and take her shopping on Fifth Avenue.

Anastasia drew the dwarf pony closer to her ample chest, then paused to take in her surroundings. Her almond-shaped brown eyes darted between the house and the ocean. Finally they settled on Massie, who was now standing directly in front of her.

"I'm Anastasia Brees," she stated, her voice low and soft and barely audible. She extended her supple hand. Massie took it, trying not to buckle under the weight of the giant amethyst on her middle finger.

"Massie Block," she offered coolly, mimicking the VIG's collected tone. "And this is Bean," she told Muse.

Gently, Anastasia placed her calf-high pony on the grass.

"Be free," Anastasia whispered to her. Muse fluttered her lips in response and pranced off with delight to wander the grounds.

Massie lowered Bean and whispered something in *her* ear, as if they too had a silent mode of communication. And luckily, off Bean went, run-yapping toward Muse.

"What an *ah*-dorable dog," Anastasia said softly as she glided toward the pool, her dress billowing. She dipped a mauve-painted toe in the water. "Has she ever done any modeling?"

Muse and Bean lapped at the purified water with their tiny pink tongues.

"Bean would be perfect for my new ad campaign," Anastasia offered, padding over to an ivory chaise. Her wet toe print left a trail Massie wished she could somehow save.

"I'm about to launch a line of—" She stopped herself and invited Massie to lean in with a flash of her mauve-polished nails. Massie got so close she could smell the sweet Be Fruity body oil warming Anastasia's blemish-free skin.

"Pet nail polish," she finished in a low whisper. "I've been testing colors on Muse. She wears hot pink extremely well."

"You can call it *neeeigh*-l polish." Massie giggled.

"Cute." Anastasia smiled, revealing perfect Dentyne-white teeth. "I'll use that."

"Of course." Massie nodded. "Maybe you could use my horse Brownie as a model too. He's so ah—"

"Is he a mini?" Anastasia crossed her toned legs.

"No, but he's—"

"Minis only," Anastasia insisted with a pity-laced grin. "Now, Massie . . ." Anastasia sat up straight in her lounge chair and slipped on a pair of gold aviators with purple lenses. "I'm not in the habit of paying personal visits to salesgirls."

Massie quickly searched the desolate grounds. *Why wasn't anyone around to witness this?*

"I'm here," she continued, "because in less than a week you've become the highest seller in Be Pretty *history*." She casually tucked some hair behind her right ear.

And there it was. Peeking out at Massie. Framed in silky blackness.

The legendary purple streak.

Massie's skin prickled. She felt like she was looking onto the eyes of Gawd. And He was looking back. Blessing her with a lifetime supply of fabulous.

"I don't know what to say," she murmured.

"Say you're free this Saturday at one o'clock." Anastasia let her hair fall back into place. "I want to throw a BPC luncheon in your honor at the Southampton Country Club."

Massie nearly rolled off her lounge chair. "I'm in." She twirled a lock of soon-to-be-purple hair around her index finger and yanked it tight.

Anastasia clapped her hands together firmly. "Then it's all set." She stood in one elegant, flowing movement and smoothed her dress. "Just e-mail your client list and we'll take care of the rest."

"Client list?"

"Don't worry—no one is going to poach your customers.

We need it for the video tribute." She snapped her fingers once and Muse galloped over.

Bean followed, yapping frantically at Anastasia's feet.

"Video tribute?" Massie asked, her mind racing. Was this the kind of video tribute they had at the Oscars to honor a dead alpha actor? Or the kind they had on VH1 where makeup artists and C-list comedians talked about someone famous as if they were total besties? Not that it mattered. Both were beyond acceptable.

Anastasia scooped up Muse and began walking toward the helicopter. Massie followed. "I want to get a few quotes from some of your clients talking about how you used our feel-good philosophy to help promote the line. If done right, it can be a real tearjerker. When a POTO helps a POTI, it can be life altering."

"Potto and a potty?" Massie's Be Plucky brows furrowed.

"Pretty On The Outside," Anastasia explained, pointing to Massie. "And Pretty On The Inside—your clients. You've helped so many girls fall in love with themselves despite their imperfections, and that's a very special thing. You've built up their self-esteem by using kindness. It's really quite moving." Anastasia stepped inside the bronze helicopter and slid on her goggles. "So get me that list and prepare to be honored for your compassion."

Anastasia pulled the door shut, started the engine, and bid farewell by making a *B* with her fingers.

Massie stood firm against the blasting winds and deafening staccato of the revving propeller. Seconds later, the chopper lift-hovered above the lawn, tilted left, and then zoomed away. Another flurry of purple glitter fell from the sky.

As the shimmering flecks gathered on her scalp, Massie started to wonder if maybe her sales technique wasn't *exactly* what Anastasia had envisioned.

But she was too elated to stress about it. After all, Anastasia had called her a POTO! And for now, that was the only thing that mattered.

CURRENT STATE OF THE UNION

IN	OUT
Makeover parties	Sleepover parties
Being a top seller	Being a top buyer
POTI (A2A)*	POTO (A2A)*

---

*A2A=According to Anastasia—nawt Massie. Yet Massie would pretend to believe in POTI until she had her purple streak. But not a single minute more.

Southampton's picturesque Main Street was bustling with stylish women swinging tissue-stuffed shopping bags from one chic boutique to the next. Luxury SUVs stood parked along the curb and clogged the narrow roads. The morning gloom had cleared to another flawless day, and, thanks to Massie's recent success, Kendra had arranged a three-hour visit with Massie's old friend Visa so they could buy an outfit for the luncheon.

Confidence oozed from Massie's tiny pores as she strolled beside her mother wearing a blousy peach Halston kimono top from the vintage closet over last year's gray Marc by Marc Jacobs short shorts. Even in old clothes she owned this town.

They brushed past a college-aged brunette wearing high-waisted dungaree jean shorts. "What a *waist*." Massie giggled.

"Sweetie!" Kendra giggle-nudged her daughter with a mix of amusement and disgrace. "What if she hears you?"

"She'd thank me," Massie muttered. "Just like everyone else I helped."

"I have a feeling that the Be Pretty philosophy does not involve making fun of people."

98

Massie rummaged through her pewter Botkier tote searching for a distraction. Ever since Anastasia had told this POTO about being kind to POTIs, Massie had felt slightly on edge. Did Anastasia really think people with bad style were pretty on the inside? Or was it just *her* way of selling makeup to the masses? Because if she did believe it, she'd probably take issue with Massie's unorthodox sales technique. And that might affect Massie's BPC alpha status and her video tribute and her purple streak and—*STOP!*

After a quick hair toss, Massie managed to erase these stressful thoughts from her head. Worrying wouldn't solve anything. It would only put a damper on Visa Day and her sunny complexion—two things she wanted to enjoy for as long as possible.

Kendra checked her gold Cartier timepiece "I just want to stop in on Horst Fishbeck at the gallery. I ordered six garden sculptures weeks ago and they haven't arrived—unless he sold them to someone else, which is exactly what I'm going to find out." She picked up her pace. "It won't take long. And then we can spend the rest of the day on you."

Massie sighed. She had to get to Intermix before her Chanel No. 19 faded and her blush was absorbed. It was crucial for her self-esteem that she shop while she looked and felt her best. And right now she was a nine. But by the time her mother got through with Horst, her blood sugar would have dropped to unsalvageable levels and her daily beauty high would dip dangerously low.

"How about I meet you for lunch." Massie checked her

reflection in the window of Agnes B. as they passed. The Halston she'd borrowed from her mother was flattering on her tiny frame, but come *awn*! Her exfoliated skin was itching to be wrapped in something designed *after* she was born.

"I don't want you shopping alone." Kendra pushed past a woman whose face was stretched so tight, she looked shocked just to be walking down the street. "Trini's neighbor's sister-in-law had her wallet stolen right out of her bag while she was lunching at Savory's."

"But I *won't* be alone." Massie hurried to keep up with her mother as she *click-clack*ed toward the gallery in her Choo slides. "I'll have Visa."

"That's not—"

"Heyyyy, you!" Lindsey Kearns called from her silver beach cruiser. She slammed on the brakes, hopped off, and lifted the bike onto the sidewalk. Her frizz was completely gone and her green eyes were lined in gray, just like Massie taught her. She had even abandoned the masculine surf trunks for a pink Roxy tank dress covered in hearts.

A feeling of pride pricked the bottoms of Massie's feet. She stomped her BCBG wood wedges against the pavement for relief.

"Lindsey, you look great," Kendra gushed, motioning for her to walk with them because she was late.

"Thanks." Lindsey rolled the silver bike beside Massie. "Your daughter did it."

Kendra stopped for a second. She covered her heart with

her jeweled hand and admired Massie as if *she* were one of Horst Fishbeck's precious works of art. Then she started walking again.

"I'm glad you're enjoying your beauty." Massie beamed.

"I am, and don't worry—that's *exactly* what I told the film crew yesterday."

"Film crew?" Kendra asked, sliding a diamond peace-sign pendant across the platinum chain around her neck.

"Yeah, Be Pretty is interviewing my clients about their makeover experience," Massie said, as if that kind of thing happened to her twice a day. "It's for the luncheon."

"What did you tell them?" Kendra asked outside the gallery, where she paused to tighten the thin gold belt on her RL navy shirtdress.

"I told them how honest Massie was." Lindsey threw a leg back over her bike seat and lifted herself up to sit. "They seemed a little shocked when I told them you said I needed a humidifier because my hair was sucking the moisture out of the room but—"

"You *told* them that?" Massie snapped at Lindsey.

"You *said* that?" Kendra snapped at Massie.

"It's okay, we're not upset." Lindsey absentmindedly rang her bell. "Anymore."

"*We're?*" Massie screeched, avoiding her mother's questioning eyes. "Who's 'we'?"

"All the other girls you helped." Lindsey smacked a deep-conditioned blond tendril away from her glistening lips. "Don't worry, after we told the camera crew what you said about us, we made sure to let them know how grateful we were for your honesty. And for promising that Be Cosmetics would make us pretty, even though God couldn't."

Kendra turned to her daughter, her proud smile fading faster than Massie's Chanel No. 19.

Massie pulled a Sony camcorder out of a metallic purple gift bag and read the card aloud. *To help you remember an unforgettable day x o x, AB,* was written in elegant purple script.

"How thoughtful." Kendra blotted her Be Berry lipstick on a linen country club napkin, then folded it into a tiny square. They sat perched on a peony pink settee, waiting for Massie to be announced to the main dining room, where the Be Pretty luncheon was already getting started.

"See, Mom, I *told* you she's not mad." Massie beamed. "Like Dad said this morning, she's a businesswoman. As long as I'm making her rich, she's happy." She waved at the camera as proof.

Finally satisfied, Kendra stood up and smoothed her cassis Dana Buchman bubble dress. "All right, then." She kissed her daughter on the forehead, enveloping her in a heady cloud of Trésor. "I'm going to find your father. I'll see you out there. Good luck, my favorite top seller."

Massie rolled her eyes. "Thanks, Mom."

The second Kendra left, Massie turned the camera lens on herself and pressed the red RECORD button.

"You'll never believe where I am right now," she said to the camera, and then panned the VIP holding room, hoping to give the Pretty Committee a glimpse into her glamorous new world. She made sure to capture the gold Lurex curtains that shimmer-hung from the walls, the chic Jonathan Adler floor vases teeming with electric purple irises, and the marble coffee table stocked with chocolate-dipped berries, Perrier, and a sampling of latte drinks.

She turned the camera back to herself. "This isn't even the actual luncheon. This is just where one of Anastasia's assistants asked me to hang until they were ready to announce me." She bit her bottom lip to keep her extreme rapture in check. "Now for the moment you've all been waiting for."

She panned over her lavender Vince trapeze dress with the skinny bronze sash that glimmered just below her A-cups, down past her spray-tanned legs, and finally to her bloodred Prada wedges.

"I've been working a whole footwear-clash thing lately. It's perfect for summer. But I'll be done with it by fall, so don't bother." She lifted the lens to her face. "Whaddaya think?"

Massie widened the shot. "Jakkob came over this morning and straightened my hair. He also applied a dark brown wash. You like?" She ran her free hand through her silky blowout. "I know it's more of a back-to-school tone, but I thought the purple streak would really pop against a rich background, and I don't want a single person to miss it. FYI: The first thing I'm going to do is get off the Intermix waiting list and get that pair of D&G sunglasses I signed up for before horse camp. The second is get a dwarf pony, and the third is buy an impossible-to-get tangerine Birkin bag to put him in."

Massie was about to ask them to rate her when the door clicked open. She immediately shut off the camera.

"Hi, I'm Katsura," said a petite woman wearing a purple lab coat and a Be Prepared makeup holster clipped to her waist. Her dark eyes scanned Massie's visage as she spoke. "I'm here to do some last-minute touch-ups on you before you go out there but"—she clutched Massie's chin and angled her face toward the light—"I can see you don't need any." She exhaled some curiously strong Altoid breath. "You did this yourself?"

Massie nodded yes, wishing the camera had been rolling.

"Very nice." Katsura turned on the heel of her three-inch gold Louboutin sandal and left out the open door. "She's all set," she announced to whoever was lurk-waiting for her in the hallway.

Major flutters erupted behind Massie's abs. Her throat locked. Her lips dried. And her palms self-moisturized. Just outside these VIP walls was a room full of makeup moguls waiting to honor her. And when they were done, she'd have lifelong access to the inaccessible. The only thing missing was the Pretty Committee. And Brownie. But she'd be sure to share every detail with them once she was anointed.

"Ready?" asked a twentysomething girl with short curly blond hair.

"Yup." Massie exhaled. She rubbed her hands together to warm her icy fingertips.

The girl pressed her black headset against her ear, straining to hear her cue. "Okay. Let's move!" She gripped Massie's arm and led her down a coral-carpeted corridor that smelled like a mix of chicken noodle soup and gardenias.

Before Massie had a chance to reapply her gloss, she was thrust into a bright, sun-soaked banquet room, inside which purple glitter was raining down.

"Introducing BPC's top seller of all time. She's beautiful on the inside *and* the outside—Miss Massie Block!" Anastasia announced into a lipstick-shaped microphone. A gold Grecian-style dress hung from one bronze-dusted shoulder. Her signature black bob had been slicked into a tight bun, offering hints of purple if examined from the proper angle. Her feet, as always, were bare.

The guests rose out of their gold velvet chairs and applauded. Proud smiles lit their faces. But no one looked prouder than William and Kendra Block, standing beside Anastasia at the head table, dabbing their eyes as their daughter walked to the front of the room to the sultry beat of Gwen Stefani's "Cool."

Fifteen cube-shaped video monitors descended from the ceiling, one above each of the mirrored tables. *Queen Be* appeared on the screens in a purple swirling font.

Somehow, despite her trembling legs, Massie managed a sincere smile when she passed un-frizzy Lindsey, acne-free Cathie, freckle-free Marin, and all the other girls she'd rehabilitated.

As rehearsed, Anastasia handed Massie a shimmering gold

makeup caddy with *MB* engraved on the clasp. They shook hands, smiled for the photographer, and lowered themselves into a purple double throne, from which they looked out at their adoring public.

Muse scurried up the plush armrests and licked Massie's cheek. She hugged him once for the camera and a second time for herself. Everyone took their seats, but kept their eyes on her. And it felt so right.

Anastasia stood. Her regal posture and gold dress made her look like an Academy Award. She held the lipstick mic below her shimmering mouth and began her address in her usual low, measured tone. "Not since *me* has a young woman sold so much to so many in so little time." She paused for applause.

Massie looked down and twirled her charm bracelet to keep from revealing her overwhelming joy. But truth be told, even her intestines were smiling.

"And I want you to know that by spreading the Be Pretty philosophy, Massie Block is helping a generation of young women *embrace* their imperfections. Not *erase* them. Because after all, isn't that what makes each one of us so special?"

Just then, table seven burst into an "Embrace, don't erase" chant. The West Coast high seller with abnormally large ears pounded her glitter-covered table. Soon, everyone followed suit.

"Embrace, don't erase! Embrace, don't erase! Embrace, don't erase!"

Massie moved her lips in time with theirs, but her brain

was in major rewind mode. Desperately, she searched her memory, trying to determine whether her feedback had fallen into the "embrace" category or the "erase" category. A niggling feeling in her stomach told her she might have said a thing or two to a client or two that maybe could have possibly qualified as an "erase." . . .

But then again, worrying about it would only bring on premature frown lines. And besides, Anastasia seemed more than pleased with her. So the video must have turned out better than great.

"Embrace, don't erase! Embrace, don't erase! Embrace, don't erase!"

"But why listen to me?" Anastasia broke in, and the chanting immediately subsided. "When you can hear it from the girls themselves."

The lights dimmed, and heavy purple blinds rolled down and covered the windows. The waitstaff quickly emerged from the kitchen delivering popcorn shrimp to the guests. Then the familiar deep-voiced narrator from the movie trailers began.

"In a small beach town rife with insecurity, there lived a girl . . ."

Anastasia leaned in and whispered, "I am so excited to see this."

Massie froze. Then began sweating. Then her vision blurred. *Anastasia hadn't seen it yet?* Her eyes darted around the room in search of the nearest exit, but all she saw were hundreds of people nibbling on popcorn shrimp, captivated by the video that was about to change her life for the better . . . or worse.

A close-up image of Lindsey Kerns leaning against a red surfboard on the beach appeared on the cubes.

"Ow, owwww!" Lindsey hooted.

Kimmi whistled through her teeth.

Massie forgot how to breathe.

Video Lindsey smiled boldly into the camera, her oil-infused locks tumbling over smoky gray-shadowed green eyes. "Massie Block showed me what beauty *really* means," she said confidently.

Anastasia's pleased grin glowed in the light reflecting from the screen.

"She taught me that beauty *is* actually skin deep and that my 'beauty' was dry and flaky," Video Lindsey continued. "Massie said I needed more coverage on the top"—she pointed to her heavily concealed face—"and less on the bottom." She wiggled her thong bikini bottom for the camera. "And she promised that if I bought the Be Pretty Cosmetics line, I'd totally find a boyfriend."

The crowd snickered. Lindsey looked down and bit her lip, looking like she might cry.

Massie side-peeked at Anastasia, afraid of what she might see. But the Be Pretty CEO was still grinning with joy. Massie breathed a Be Minty–scented sigh of relief. William must have been right. The whole "inner beauty" thing was just a hook to sell more product. All she cared about was the bottom line.

Thank Gawd!

Lindsey's grinning image faded to a shot of Marin, posing by her pool in a white sundress. Massie had to admit the ol' freckle-face looked good for her. She flashed a thumbs-up at Marin and her mother, sitting just a few tables away. They smiled back.

"Massie told me freckles and heavy prints can induce nausea. So I donated my entire wardrobe to Darfur and replaced it with solids. Then I got a laser facial. Oh, and I also use Be Flawless foundation." The camera zoomed in on Marin's face, and she winked. "Thanks, Massie. Without you, I'd never have known the truth about my nauseating looks."

Marin's mom slammed down her gold-rimmed glass. She was waving her hands and mouthing something to Massie, but Massie couldn't quite make it out. Again, Massie side-peeked at her mentor, but Anastasia was still grinning.

"Normally when someone calls your embarrassing black-head and whitehead condition a 'nose full of salt and pepper' it's upsetting," said Video Cathie while swinging in her porch swing. Her face had been scrubbed raw. "But my pores *were* super clogged. Now my acne is gone . . . along with the top layer of my skin. But who cares? It was worth it, don'tcha think?" She caressed her red nose.

Anastasia's eyes were glued to the video while her thumbs sent a quick text. Seconds later, one of her many purple lab coat–wearing assistants appeared with her metallic gold makeup holster. She snapped the chic fanny pack around the waist of her flowing gown, then dismissed the assistant with a stiff half-nod. Massie side-stared at the holster in awe.

Six pockets hung off the belt, each one stuffed with products from Be's high-end, special-edition Gold line. Each brush, shadow, pencil, balm, and gloss was wrapped in a gilt-plated package.

Except for one. It was the shape of a Crayola marker and the color of an eggplant. And it stood alone. In all its purple glory.

Massie instantly sat on her hands to keep them from shaking. On the video Noelle was saying something about an earthquake in Sephora, but it was impossible to concentrate. Greatness was an arm's length away. And she found herself trembling in its presence. Was this how Lauren Conrad felt when she met Marc Jacobs on *The Hills*?

"Come with me," Anastasia whisper-grinned. She placed Muse in her Fendi wooly-fringe-and-feather "To You" bag and stood.

Massie choked back a "Yay!" as she hurry-followed her mentor out the side exit, reveling in the jealous looks and excited whispers of everyone they passed. This was it! The moment she had slaved for all week. Anastasia was going to take that purple marker out of her holster and paint Massie into her exclusive club. And then they would reenter the luncheon as in-the-know equals and make mini-pony-shopping plans as soon as the guests cleared out.

Once they were alone in the VIP holding room, Anastasia shut the door behind them. She opened her Fendi on the floor and smiled peacefully as Muse trotted out and began galloping around the marble coffee table.

Massie's stomach fluttered in anticipation. She tried her hardest to look unsuspecting, but it was too late. The I-know-I'm-about-to-get-a-purple-streak grin had already settled on her face.

And it held strong . . . until Anastasia explained why they were really there.

Without a single word, Anastasia lowered herself onto the edge of the peony pink settee. The Be Elite purple pen jiggled around in its holster as she tried to get comfortable. But Anastasia didn't reach for it. Instead, she pulled out a handful of products and popped open her Be Reflective compact. With the finesse of an artist, she dabbed Be Peachy blush on the apples of her cheeks, traced her dark eyes with Be Money green glitter pencil, and double glossed her lips with a bottom coat of Be Pink and a top coat of Be Flashy. It was like watching Picasso paint, only fun.

"My *Gawd*, you're ugly!" Anastasia snapped her mirrored compact shut and stood.

"Ehmagawd, you are so *nawt*—" Massie started, reaching for the chocolate-dipped fruit.

"Not *me*!" She whacked the strawberry out of Massie's hand. *"You!"*

Massie giggled. This had to be some sort of purple-streak initiation joke. After all, Anastasia had called her a POTO just a couple days ago. But the mogul turned away in disgust. She faced the gold Lurex curtains and lowered her head.

"Wait." Panic-sweat prickled its way through Massie's tiny pores and dampened her forehead. "You're not kidding?"

Anastasia shook her head no.

"You seriously think I'm *ugly*?" The room started spinning. It was hard to know where Anastasia's Oscar-statue dress began and the curtains ended. Massie felt like a cardboard cone swirling around a giant vat of gold cotton candy.

"Ugly?"

"Yes." Anastasia turned to face Massie, her almond-shaped eyes glistening with tears. "On the *inside*."

The spinning room settled.

"Phew." Massie fanned her forehead. "So I'm still pretty on the outside, right?"

"What difference does *that* make?" Anastasia scooped up Muse and held him close. "You told those girls how *unattractive* they were."

"Key word, *were*," Massie reminded her patiently. "Now they're so much less unattractive. Thanks to us."

"No!" Anastasia shook her head and set down the mini horse. "You missed the entire point of Be Pretty Cosmetics! You completely misrepresented my brand! And now those poor girls out there are more damaged than ever."

Massie slumped back down on the pink chaise and hid her burning cheeks in Muse's mane. All she wanted to do was succeed. And now she was being looked at as a total failure. Even though her face was covered, Massie could feel Anastasia's disappointed glare as clearly as she had felt Brownie's. And it hurt more than laser hair removal.

"I'm so sorry." Massie placed a reassuring hand on Anastasia's perfectly moisturized shoulder. "I honestly had no idea you *believed* all that beauty-on-the-inside stuff."

Anastasia lifted her eyes and knit her perfectly arched brows, her sadness morphing suddenly into anger. "Well, what *did* you think? That I spent the last seven years of my life developing a cosmetics line and attending self-esteem seminars just so I could end up on *People*'s Most Beautiful list?"

"Well, yeah." Massie shrugged.

"Well, wrong!" Anastasia stood again. "Being overly attractive is a gift. And I intend to use my gift to inspire others. Not prey on their insecurities for money. You should be ashamed of yourself."

Anastasia irritably adjusted her makeup holster. The purple streaking pen slid just out of Massie's view.

"I'm really sorry," Massie mumbled to the hem of her purple dress. The last thing she wanted to do was let Anastasia down. Well, actually that was the second to last thing. The last thing she wanted to do was be a low seller. "I just wanted to make you proud." She sniffled. "Because you're my"—she sniffled again—"role model."

Anastasia offered Massie a withering look and marched over to the door.

Massie blotted the corner of her eye with a silver cocktail napkin and watched her go. What would she tell her parents? Her friends? Her customers? Her *hair*? And then she realized something. Something huge. And that something had to be taken care of if she ever wanted to look in the mirror again and feel proud.

"No, wait!" She hurried to Anastasia's side and grabbed her wrist just as she was about to turn the handle. "What can I do to make it up to you?"

Anastasia's expression softened. "For starters, you can apologize to everyone in that room."

"Done." Massie smiled gratefully and ran a finger under her tear-soaked eyes.

"And promise you will work on your inner beauty."

"Done." Massie smiled again. "I guess I was so desperate to be your top seller I lost track of who *you* really are. Aaaand all of the important things you stand for."

Anastasia closed her eyes and exhaled. "Thank you for saying that."

Massie held out her arms and batted her lashes like a timid fawn. "Forgive me?" She sniffled, then hugged her mentor.

"I'll try." Anastasia smirked, returning the gesture.

After a heartfelt embrace, Anastasia pulled away and locked eyes with Massie. "You know, being on top feels better if you can look down and know you didn't step on anyone during your climb."

Massie dabbed the corners of her eyes one last time . . . pretending to agree.

They reentered the terrace just as the tribute video was wrapping up. The final shot was a scrolling list of Massie's unprecedented sales record set to the tune of Christina Aguilera's "Beautiful." When the song ended, the screen went dark and the room erupted in a frenzy of applause.

Anastasia's shellacked mouth dropped open.

Almost everyone gave Massie a standing ovation, except a few of the mothers who shook their heads and glared at Kendra as if she were somehow responsible. But Kendra ignored them, choosing to clap and cheer with the rest of the guests.

"Excuse me?" Anastasia said crisply. "Can I have your attention please?"

One of her purple lab coat–wearing assistants quickly handed her the lipstick microphone. Anastasia smiled her thank-you, then continued. "Please hold your applause. Massie has something she would like to say."

Everyone sat and smiled expectantly.

Suddenly Massie's stomach lurched. Did Anastasia seriously expect her to *apologize* to these people? For *what*? Making them attractive?

"Massie rules!" Lindsey shouted from her table.

Everyone applauded again.

Like a seasoned professional, Massie stood at the front of the room, happy to let their adoration run its course.

"Unbelievable," Anastasia muttered under her breath. She lifted her palm, requesting silence. "Go ahead." She nudged Massie.

But Massie was speechless. Her inner alpha was hiding, refusing to participate in a public apology.

Instead, she glanced out at the smiling faces staring back at her—many of them faces she'd single-handedly transformed from gruesome to gorgeous without the help of even one dermatologist or plastic surgeon. And how could that *Be* wrong?

"Speak," Anastasia hissed.

"Um," Massie tried. "I wanted to let you all know that I'm really sorr—" She stopped herself just in time. "I'm really honored to have served you. But I'm retiring."

"What?" Anastasia gasped. "That's not what you're—"

"I know you're shocked," she blurted. "But my work here is done."

"Truth is beauty!" shouted Cathie.

Everyone whoo-hooed.

Massie giggled modestly and then continued. "You all look ah-mazing, *on the outside*. And now, the inside part is up to you. Thanks for helping me become number one. Enjoy your beauty!" She handed Anastasia the mic, waved goodbye to her protégées, and hurried for the exit like a pop star hounded by the paparazzi.

Anastasia called after her, but Massie refused to stop. Why bother? Her commission check had cleared two days ago. She'd paid her parents back. And she was the Be Pretty Cosmetics number one seller of all time. She'd gotten everything she wanted.

Everything. ☺

Massie strolled down Main Street with her mother and openly applied two generous coats of Vanilla Espresso Bean–flavored Glossip Girl to her lips. Finally! No more hiding. The days of pretending Be Shiny lip gloss was more moisturizing were over.

"I'm ready." Massie tightened the knot on her silk Pucci hair wrap and checked her Marc by Marc Jacobs orange wide-strap watch for the millionth time that morning. "Two minutes before they open."

"Okay." Kendra pulled a vellum envelope out of her navy Chanel clutch. "Here you go."

Massie tore it open, desperate for what was inside. "Yes!" she shouted, and then gave the silver Visa a big glossy kiss. "Mwah! Welcome home."

Kendra pushed back the sleeves on her white Catherine Malandrino shirtdress with a pleased smile. "You deserve it. Your father and I are very proud of you."

The compliments were nice, but all Massie really wanted to hear was, "Come on in," from the manager at Intermix. And she would, in exactly fifty-eight seconds, when the trendy store opened.

"I never imagined you'd be able to pay us back for Galwaugh

in a week." Kendra finger-swatted her blowout away from her face. "We are so impressed with—"

The glass door clicked open, allowing a gust of chilly air to rush out of the all-white store and blow by Massie's face like a floral-scented burp.

"Thanks, Mom, I'll meet you at Savory's for lunch in forty-five minutes," Massie said to a jewel toned dress–wearing mannequin in the window.

"Sounds great—have fun." Kendra *click-clack*ed off to buy a new tennis outfit.

Massie checked her reflection in the window, knowing she was about to make a very big impression on some very small people. She'd paired a turquoise Thread Social mini dress with flat gold Prada thong sandals and white drop earrings.

"Ten," she said to herself with a giddy giggle, and then entered.

With an eye on the blond pixie working the register, Massie marched past the tidy silver racks of Chloé, Mint, Ella Moss, and Theory. She had all summer for those. All she needed now were her sunglasses. The kind Nicole Richie wore by the pool in Vegas over Memorial Day weekend. The kind everyone tried to get after they saw her picture in *US Weekly*. The kind that Massie tried to get before Galwaugh.

The kind that had a list.

"Can I help you?" asked the salesgirl without looking up from her article on Brad and Angelina's latest adoptee.

"A pair of gold-framed oversize gold D&G sunglasses, please. Style code c-71—"

"Don't bother." The girl slid a clipboard across the counter. A stack of coffee-stained pages were sloppily attached.

"Enteryournameemailaddresscellphonenumber.We'llcallyouwhenwegetmore." She clicked a pink Intermix pen and slammed it down on the stack.

"I'm already on the list," Massie informed her.

"Then we'll call you if they come in." The girl flipped a page in *US Weekly* and yawned.

"You don't understand." Massie pushed the clipboard aside. "You can take me off the list and just give me the glasses. And don't bother with a bag. I'll be wearing them home."

The salesgirl finally looked up. "You're looking at a five-year wait. I couldn't get you those glasses even if my name was Ivanka." She gave Massie a searing once-over.

Just then, a skinny blond salesguy burst through the front door of the store like he was making his Broadway debut and quickly put on a headset. "Sorry I'm laaaaaate. Mandy Moore was on Martha talking about how comfortable she is being a size eight and you know what a sucker I am for a good comedy."

"You wanna laugh even harder?" the girl asked.

The salesguy, whose name tag read STEVEN, nodded as he lifted his FASHION IS EASY . . . JUST LIKE YOU T-shirt until it revealed a tuft of blond stomach hair just above his jeans. Ew.

"This girl thinks she's walking out of here with a pair of gold D&Gs."

He burst out laughing while assessing his tiny butt in the slimming wall mirror.

It was go time. Massie loosened the knot on her hair wrap, letting her glossy layers tumble to her shoulders. She stepped under a track light and tilted her head to the left, revealing an unmistakable purple streak.

The girl's angular jaw dropped.

Steven gasped.

"Code purple," he whisper-shouted into his headset. "Repeat, *code purple*." He kept his eyes fixed on Massie's streak. "It *means*, Mark, that we've got a purple streak in the store, and she wants a pair of the gold-framed D&Gs. Now *move!*" He nodded apologetically at Massie. "It'll just take a second. In fact, I'm sure Moira would be happy to run back there and speed things up a little."

"Happy to." Moira scurried to the back of the store, her red skinny jeans revealing the pink lace on her Cosabellas.

"Thaaanks, Moira," Massie giggle-called after her.

"Party Like a Rock Star" throbbed over the speakers as Steven sashayed across the store and flipped the lock on the front door. "So you can shop in peace," he explained to Massie. "Can I get you anything, Miss . . . ?"

"Block. Massie Block."

"Cappuccino?"

Massie crossed the store. "That's all for now, thank you."

She stood smiling at her own ingenuity. All it had taken was a sympathetic eyelash bat, one hug from Anastasia, and some quick fingers. And like in that old game Operation, Massie had lifted that purple pen out of its holster with extreme precision and dropped it in her bag.

"Here we are. Our very last pair." Moira returned from the back clutching a metallic bronze D&G sunglasses case. She held it out to Massie. "Is this what you wanted, miss?"

"Exactly." Massie smiled, clicking open the smooth metallic box.

She peered down at the magnificent gold-framed glasses nestled in the velvet-lined case and beamed. She lifted them out and slid them on. They felt heavy. Solid. And very, very exclusive. Massie slapped down her Visa and turned to admire herself in the round countertop accessories mirror. Her hair was swept over one shoulder and gleamed as brightly as her new frames.

Purple and gold were a winning combination—one that suited her perfectly.

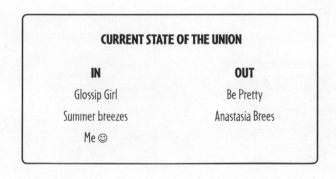

CURRENT STATE OF THE UNION

IN	OUT
Glossip Girl	Be Pretty
Summer breezes	Anastasia Brees
Me ☺	

Now that you know the secret of the streak, you're one step closer to being **IN**. In the know, that is. . . .

SUMMER STATE OF THE UNION

IN	OUT
✓ Purple hair streaks	Summer secrets
Confidentiality contracts	
Euro pop stars	
Shark-tooth necklaces	
Massie & Claire in Orlando	

Five girls. Five stories. One ah-mazing summer.

THE CLIQUE
SUMMER COLLECTION

BY LISI HARRISON

Turn the page for a sneak peek
of Dylan's story. . . .

THE CLIQUE

SUMMER COLLECTION

DYLAN

Dylan Marvil sat across from her famous mother on the *Daily Grind*'s private jet en route to a spa in Hawaii, wondering why anyone in their right mind would *choose* to fly commercial. The luxe cabin was papered with interlocking *D*'s and *G*'s; the seats were made of butter-soft tan leather; and the in-flight movie was anything she wanted it to be. The only thing missing was a silver spoon for her fat-free triple chocolate banana spilt. Thank Gawd the petite brunette in the cute navy mini dress was rushing one right over.

Dylan gratefully took the spoon and swallowed a mouthful of cold, creamy deliciousness. "Ahhh! Brain-freeze!" she shouted as the icy coldness shot straight up to her scarlet roots.

Without lifting her emerald green eyes, Merri-Lee Marvil tossed a snowy white cashmere throw on her daughter's lap and returned to her thick file on Svetlana Slootskyia, the teen tennis phenom and current *Maxim* cover girl. She reclined in her seat, tucked her burgundy blowout behind her ears, and began flipping through the research material her assistant, Cassidy Wolfe, had prepared for her upcoming interview.

Until Svetlana, the only thing tennis-related Dylan had ever noticed was the sparkling diamond bracelet glinting on her mother's wrist. But these days, "Tennis the Menace" was impossible to ignore.

At first she made headlines for her blond hotness. But then she TMZ'ed her way onto Dylan's radar when she whipped her racquet at a ball girl's teeth after losing some majorly important match. And this was only four days after she smashed her boyfriend in the mouth with a yellow Dunlop because he smile-thanked the soda girl for his Pepsi. After twelve weeks of anger management therapy, she emerged to scores of paparazzi, all of them hoping to snap *her* when she snapped again.

Now, every entertainment journalist from Maria Menounos to Nancy O'Dell was tripping over her Manolos to get a post-rehab interview with Svetlana. But it was more impossible to land than Chanel's Black Tulip nail polish, since Merri-Lee had bought the rights to the Slootskyia story the second Svetlana's Wilson KFactor collided with Ali Chipley's incisors.

"Ha! I'll show *her*," Merri-Lee blurted, scribbling something on her yellow legal pad.

"Who?" Dylan licked the silver dessert spoon and dropped it in the fat-free chocolate soup that was starting to congeal on the bottom of her crystal bowl.

"Barbara Walters. She's not the only one willing to go *there*."

It was the interview of the season, and Merri-Lee was determined to deliver high drama. But to Dylan, Svetlana was little more than a first-class ticket to five-star fat camp.

She was a celebrity-style opportunity to drop the four pounds she'd gained while trying to show Kemp Hurley and Chris Plovert that she wasn't a prissy girly girl who fussed over calories. Even though she was.

After a short snooze and a steaming lavender-scented face towel, Dylan threw the blanket off her emerald green Juicy puff-sleeved hoodie and, out of pure boredom, reached for a stack of Merri-Lee's research materials. She scanned the headlines next to various photographs of Svetlana petting her thick side-braid. BLOND BOMBSHELL EXPLODES . . . BALL GIRL'S TEETH SOLD ON EBAY . . . NIKE SWOOSHES TO SVETLANA'S RESCUE WITH AN ENDORSEMENT DEAL. . . .

Dylan flipped through dozens of pictures and then sighed hopelessly. Every picture showed Svetlana in some bland white dress and athletic sneakers. Suhhh-noooozer!

"Mom, do you think there will be anyone my age who's *not* into tennis?"

"Cass!" Merri-Lee called back to her assistant, ignoring her daughter. "Are we confirmed on all of Svetlana's must-haves?"

Cassidy unbuckled her gold *DG*-stamped seat belt and appeared between Merri-Lee and Dylan on the brocade-carpeted aisle. Her auburn curls were pinch-clamped to the back of her head by a clear Scunci jaw clip.

"Spirulina detox smoothies, all the recent tabloids with all photos of Paris Hilton removed, thirty packs of orange Tic Tacs, Tocca candles in lemon verbena, unscented baby wipes instead of toilet paper, and a gray kitty cat with haunting blue eyes." She tapped her pad with the tip of her pencil. "We're all set."

"Fan-tastic."

Cassidy turned on her ivory espadrilles and wobble-bounced back to her seat.

Suddenly, the plane dipped. It quickly recovered, but the sinking feeling in Dylan's stomach remained. Was she doomed to spend her spa vacation watching her mother kiss some blond Russian's ultra-toned butt? Gawd! Just because *she* wasn't famous or blond or toned or violent didn't mean she deserved to be ignored.

"Aloha. We will now begin our initial descent into Honolulu. They had quite a thunderstorm last night, so everything will be beautiful and fresh for your arrival. . . ." The pilot's smooth voice sent an anxious ripple through Dylan's undefined abs.

Ehmagawd! Fresh! It was time to make a fresh start.

No more comparing herself to Svetlana, or *anyone*. The next three weeks would be all about *Dylan* learning to love Dylan. No more super-skinny Westchester girls to compete with. No more alphas to obey. No more pretending to be someone she wasn't. No more crushing on boys who didn't crush back. Starting now, Dylan's raison d'être would be about making summer goals and reaching them. Her days of feeling inadequate were over.

And if anyone wanted to witness a real temper tantrum, all they had to do was stand in her way.

THE CLIQUE

SUMMER COLLECTION

BY LISI HARRISON

DYLAN 5/6/2008

Before Dylan and her mom check into a posh weight loss spa in Hawaii, her mom has to interview the hot-tempered tennis star, Ilana "Tennis the Mennis" Slootskyia. One furious tantrum later, Dylan has some serious blackmail material on her hands, and she plans to use it as craftily as Massie would.

poppy

www.pickapoppy.com

Available Wherever Books Are Sold

THE CLIQUE

SUMMER COLLECTION

BY LISI HARRISON

ALICIA   6/3/2008

Back in Spain visiting her family, Alicia and her cousins are forced to pay for party-related damage to hotel property with summer jobs. Alicia and Nina have been hired on as towel girls. What's worse is that Nina's hot older sisters got the sweet assignment of "Guest Relations" — lounging by the pool making chit chat with teen boys. This is nothing a little wicked scheme can't fix. *Adios, bimbos!*

poppy

www.pickapoppy.com

Available Wherever Books Are Sold

THE CLIQUE
SUMMER COLLECTION
BY LISI HARRISON

KRISTEN 7/1/2008

Stuck at OCD for the summer fulfilling scholarship commitments, Kristen takes a babysitting job on the side. The little girl is a hellion, but Kristen falls hard for her older brother, Dune. Bummer that all the time she's spending with him is making her grades fall, too.

poppy
www.pickapoppy.com

Available Wherever Books Are Sold

THE CLIQUE
SUMMER COLLECTION
BY LISI HARRISON

CLAIRE 8/5/2008

Back home in Orlando for the summer, Claire drops everything the Pretty Committee taught her and picks right back up with her LBR friends. Things are great...until Massie unexpectedly shows up. Claire is forced to pick between her two best friends. Will she risk her standing in the Pretty Committee for the sake of loyalty?

poppy
www.pickapoppy.com
Available Wherever Books Are Sold